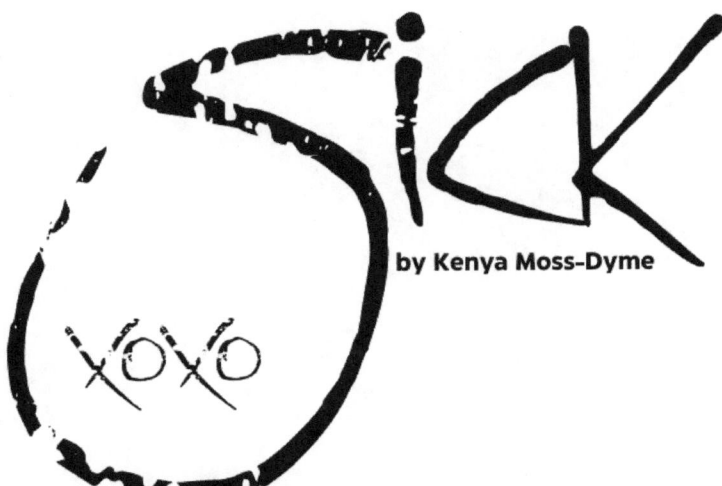

Sick

by Kenya Moss-Dyme

XOXO

Dedication

Marla Jackson – I hope they have books in Heaven. "I wrote something for you, Ms. Jackson."

Sonya Brown (Sissy) – God knew to make you my only sister because if I had another, I'd push her down the stairs so you would be my only sister. Love you beyond measure.

Ebony Evans & EyeCU Reading and Chatting – Three of the stories were conceived in this "little" Facebook group during the Freestyle Friday challenges. I am so thankful for Ebony, the group and the freestyles that have helped me fine tune my craft.

Foreword

The inspiration for "Sick xoxo" (aka sick love and kisses) came from a conversation I had with my mom a very long time ago. She said to me, what is scarier than being so much in love with (a man) that you allow them access to ALL of you? Your money, your safety, your thoughts, your body; you let down all your guards and they can destroy you and leave you in a pile of ashes that blow away with the wind. What's scarier than that?

This collection of stories is about love; but then it's also about sex and death and some pretty ugly, dark and twisted fantasies about human connections. I had fun writing each one of these, and I hope you have fun reading them.

Let's get sick.
Love, Kenya

Stories

Subscribe

Subscribe and stay up to date on new releases, book events, special discounts. You'll also have the chance to be included in the monthly drawing for subscriber appreciation prizes! **Scan the QR code below, or visit my website** and click **Subscribe**!

Limbo

Just breathe, girl.
In. Out. In. Out.

Autumn shook her wrists to calm her nerves as she approached the heavy metal doors of the factory. Her first day on this job and she was already feeling so overwhelmed by the commute that she almost went back home. Now she stood at the entrance and listened to the sights and sounds - the grind of machinery, the hiss of steam, the shouts of men (and women) moving equipment. She clutched the handle of her lunch bag tightly with her left hand, wishing it was all a dream. But when her right hand closed on the cold steel door handle, she knew it was real.

She was about to work on a factory floor, and it was going to be different than anything she'd ever experienced.

As a single mother, Autumn couldn't afford to wait for better opportunities. She needed a job and this was the only one that called her for an interview. Not only an interview but they hired her on the spot. That hadn't happened to her since high school so she was determined to at least try to get a few checks, pay some bills up to date, and then move on to a job more fitting for her particular skill set. And less hazardous to her health.

She passed through two sets of security doors before reaching the reception area where she was greeted by a cheerful young girl at the desk. Introducing herself as Robette, she welcomed Autumn to Mayweather Plastics and motioned for her to follow her into the factory. Autumn was at first struck by Robette's delicate beauty, but when she fell in step behind her, she noticed that the girl's right foot was encased in a cast.

Fully aware that her hobbling lead would draw questions, Robette looked over her shoulder and quipped, "It's okay, it only hurts when I walk."

Autumn giggled to hide her nervousness as she followed Robette - slowly - through the maze of assembly lines, past enormous metal presses and fabricating machines. Her face was full of wide-eyed enthusiasm, smiling at the workers along the way, noting how focused they were as they operated their stations with such precision.

Finally, Robette stopped at a desk in the middle of the factory floor and introduced Autumn to the foreman. The noise of the machinery caused them to yell their introductions even as they leaned close. Luckily, the foreman wore a badge which identified him as Tony Millsap; he promptly reached into the desk drawer and presented Autumn with her own name tag. He tapped his chest, indicating he wanted her to affix her tag to her clothing in a similar fashion.

Tony had a friendly smile shaped by a mouth of dingy, overcrowded teeth. They pointed in every direction except straight, but together they gave him a comforting smile that helped put Autumn at ease. He nodded toward the lunch bag tucked under her arm and raised his hands to mimic a small door opening and closing - she was able to decipher that he was asking her about a locker.

"Oh, no, not yet," she replied over the din.

Tony nodded again and beckoned for her to follow as he led her toward the locker room located back near the front of the factory. Once she had her locker assigned and deposited her personal items, Tony brought her to a station where half-finished car parts were dropped onto a conveyor belt. A large LED sign handing directly behind her station read, DAYS WITHOUT INCIDENT; the bold red digital portion of the sign displayed the number 3.

"Don't worry about that," Tony said when he noticed her reading the sign. "It's to encourage accountability around here. I'm not putting you on the dangerous machines though - unless you want to?" He laughed, then turned and waved his hand toward the moving station.

"You'll be inspecting these pieces for defects and removing any bad ones," he shouted over the clamber. Autumn nodded, rolling up her sleeves as Tony lead her through a short training session before offering a fist bump and leaving her to the task.

Moving slowly at first, Autumn began to feel self-conscious as the other inspectors on the same conveyor belt seemed to be rolling their eyes at her - or perhaps it was just her imagination. It wasn't long before she caught on and then quickly fell into the tedious rhythm of inspection and sorting. Despite the noise and grease, she started to relax. She was good at this detailed kind of work; it was fairly easy and the time passed quickly.

Maybe this job wouldn't be too bad after all, she thought to herself as the lunch
time bell rang. If the make-up of the floor was
any indicator, the factory was overwhelmingly
staffed by women. Which wasn't too odd, she
guessed. Mayweather Plastics produced small
automotive parts like housings, covers and
trim pieces. While the production was high
volume, this location focused on sorting, inspecting, cleaning and packaging, so the work
was less strenuous than other plants where
they were operating the dangerous equipment.

Still, Autumn observed that a number
of women seemed to have suffered an injury
or three at some point in their lives. Seated
directly on the other side of the conveyor table
was another gorgeous black woman, perhaps
early 30s, with a closed shaved head and a tiny
diamond stud in one nostril. She wore bright
red lipstick that made her lips pop. Behind her
safety goggles she had long dark eyelashes on
one eye, and a black eyepatch on the other.

Don't stare. Don't stare. Don't-

The conveyor belt suddenly stopped
and Autumn was relieved to pull off her protective glasses. Self-consciously, she turned
her back to the one-eyed woman so she could
rub her eyes. When she opened them again,

she was startled to see that Tony was walking towards her chatting eagerly with a very handsome and tall black man.

"How's it going over here?"

With the noise lowered substantially, she was able to hear everything much more clearly. She looked past Tony, into the gentleman with the sparkling dark brown eyes and a smile that stirred something inside her.

"Going just fine, sir," Autumn answered and immediately hoped she didn't have grease smudges on her face.

"Glad to hear it. I just wanted to introduce you to Victor Mayweather. He's one of the owners of the company. Victor - this is Autumn Lawrence" Tony stepped to the side as Victor moved forward with his hand extended to Autumn. Autumn felt her legs go weak as she allowed him to envelop her hand into his warm, firm grip.

This is the most beautiful man I've ever seen, she thought to herself.

Victor was tall and broad shouldered, ex-football player, she guessed as she took in his wide neck and long arms. He had a chiseled jawline beneath a neatly trimmed beard, and thick dark eyebrows that danced above intense brown eyes and long eyelashes. She almost giggled at the contrast of the corporate-y black framed glasses on his face and the sexual energy emanating from the rest of his magnificent body. A wave of warmth rushed through her legs as she met his eyes and held on to his hand just a little too long.

"Nice to meet you, Autumn. Welcome aboard!" His voice was deep, inviting, and Autumn immediately felt an unexpected flutter in her chest as she returned his smile.

Victor released her hand and stepped back, ending their brief but intense moment.

"I look forward to working for you, Victor - is it okay if I call you Victor?" She asked."Yes, of course, Victor is fine," he replied, holding her gaze for a moment. "And likewise. "Let me know if you need anything. I hope you'll be happy here."

Could have just been a glint of light bouncing off of the machinery, but her heart fluttered a little bit at the idea of him low key flirting back. Could it have been a wink from behind those sturdy glasses?

He and Tony pivoted to the next station to repeat the introduction, and she watched Victor's butt as he walked away, imagining herself gripping those beautiful mounds of flesh while he lay between her legs. He looked back at her and her knees almost buckled. It wasn't her imagination that time, he was definitely flirting!

Just as her stomach growled, the loud bell signaled the beginning of their lunch break so Autumn broke her concentration on Victor's body and rushed to the ladies restroom.

To her surprise, she found a group of women huddled together inside of the restroom by the row of sinks. They were standing in a circle with their heads leaned in close, listening to a tale by one that was particularly animated as she waved her arms excitedly and jerked her neck from side to side. A silence fell over the room as Autumn entered; she smiled and nodded, then began to walk past each stall, pushing the doors open to select the cleanest one. She could feel the women watching her, so she settled on the last stall, furthest away from their little group.

Loud whispers and giggles rose in the air. Autumn bristled as she hurried to complete her business and exit the stall. She could feel their eyes on her as she washed her hands in the sink, so she looked directly at them because, well, she was no one's punk. They looked away when she stared them down as she rinsed.

"You looked a damn fool drooling over that man," came a voice from behind.

Autumn looked in the mirror and saw one of the women standing directly behind her. Slightly smaller in stature, she wore the same orange striped safety vest as herself.

"What?" She asked, watching her warily as the woman moved to the sink on her side.

"I said, calm your tits. He's mine anyway," She tossed her hair over her shoulder to cascade down her back. Folding her arms defiantly, she leaned a hip against the sink and fixed a stare on Autumn.

"The way you're looking at him like he's a piece of meat, it ain't becoming of an old broad."

Autumn was taken aback. She wasn't sure how to respond as she sized up the situation to determine whether the girl was joking or was she legitimately about to get into a squabble on her first day at work? She raised her eyebrow, not wanting to seem weak but also careful not to escalate things.

"I'm not sure what you mean," she replied, trying to stay calm and keep her voice even. "I'm new, I was just meeting the managers and trying to be nice."

The girl was clearly young, possibly late 20s, if Autumn had to guess. Slim and attractive, her curves were visible even behind the standard factory vest and black cargo pants. She had a cute perky nose and pouty lips that frowned as she sized up Autumn, wondering how much effort she needed to put into the conversation. The tag affixed to her vest read, "Sugar".

After a few minutes of a stare down, Sugar let out a laugh that sounded more like a snort. "Please, honey, I know that look. You're sizing him up like a piece of prime rib. He looks good, I know. But he's not interested in your washed-up ass."

"Okay, what exactly is going on right now?" Autumn demanded, feeling her cheeks flush with anger. "I don't even know who you are, but I'm not interested in your man, as you say!"

Autumn knew a threat when she smelled it, so she instinctively braced to fight, in case Sugar made a leap in her direction. Instead, Sugar turned on the water and began washing her hands.

"You might not be interested but I know that look in his eye. And I don't appreciate outsiders coming in trying to steal what's mine," she said, staring at Autumn in the mirror.

This girl had to be pulling her leg, Autumn thought, there was no way that a man like Victor would be involved with the likes of her. He was classy, he was professional and she looked like one of those social media models that also sold waist trainers online.

"I didn't realize he was off-limits," she said sarcastically. "Maybe you should put a ring on it next time."

Sugar laughed loudly then turned and pumped the handle of the paper towel dispenser. She continued staring at Autumn as she dried her hands then leaned over to deposit the soiled napkin in the trash can against the wall between them.

As Autumn stepped back to allow her access, she noticed that Sugar was missing both baby fingers. Her hands were awkwardly shaped and the missing digits made Sugar's hands resemble tiny rodent paws. Uncomfortable now, Autumn focused on drying her own hands to avoid looking at Sugar's obvious disability.

Moments after all of the women followed Sugar out of the bathroom, the door to one of the stalls opened and a busty brunette stopped at the sink next to Autumn.

"Don't worry, she's harmless. Her name might be Sugar but she ain't too sweet!" The woman said loudly, catching Autumn's eye in the mirror.

"Thanks," replied Autumn. "I know I'm the new girl so I'm gonna get a little shit."

The woman pumped soap into her hand and leaned over to rinse beneath the faucet. She flipped her long hair behind her shoulder and tilted her head to the side, revealing a crisscross patch of gauze and tape where her right ear should be. Maybe the ear was still there, buried beneath the bandages, but Autumn felt uneasy looking at it, and she damn sure wasn't going to talk to it.

She smiled politely and hurried out of the bathroom.

Autumn's hands were slightly shaking as she made her way to the cafeteria. Sugar had certainly rattled her but she was determined to not let that ruin her impression of the job. Perhaps Sugar was nursing a little crush on the boss man the same as herself, but Sugar seemed so confident in her position that either she was delusional...or she was telling the truth. If she were telling the truth then that meant Autumn actually had a shot with Victor! She giggled to herself when she realized that either way, this was actually good news.

As she crossed the factory floor, she saw Victor still moving about chatting with the workers. Autumn watched as he moved down the line, and she couldn't help but notice the way he carried himself, so confident and charming. She couldn't deny that she was drawn to him in a way that she hadn't felt since she met her Geraldo, her ex-husband. That kind of intense attraction burned fast and hot, but left her in emotional turmoil when it fizzled out. She swallowed hard and shook her head to stop the flood of ugly memories from *that* time in her life when she loved a bit too hard.

She sat at a table in a corner of the bustling cafeteria area, while Victor and Tony sat a few tables away, laughing with other managers and supervisors, according to the business shirts and pencil holders in their chest pockets. Victor caught her eye once and smiled. Autumn's heart did a little flip.

She scolded herself - he was her boss, nothing more. But as the week went by, she found herself daydreaming about his smile, his eyes, his voice. Sometimes she imagined them together outside of work, sitting in her living room watching Netflix; walking through the mall hand in hand as they window shopped, or sitting together at the Japanese steakhouse, giggling as they watched the chef work his magic on the hot grill. It was ridiculous, she knew, just a silly crush. Still, she lived for those moments when he would stop to ask how she was doing, resting his hand lightly on her arm as they spoke.

By Friday, Autumn's crush had bloomed into full-blown infatuation. She laughed giddily as she got ready for work, eager to see Victor again. This job was turning out to be so much more than just a paycheck. She only hoped he felt the same spark she did.

Monday was so far away.

───*ℓℓ*───

The phone rang too many times.

It always made her nervous when he took too long to answer. She worried that one day he would not answer at all. But he always did.

Sleep in his voice, he answered in his usual gruff tone but the sound of his voice was soothing.

"What is it?"

Autumn chuckled. "Well, good evening to you too."

"I was sleeping. It's nighttime."

"I know, I'm sorry. I just got off. Thinking about Brian, wanted to call."

Deep sigh.

"You just got off? New job?"

"Yeah, started today. At Mayweather Plastics. Remember it?"

"That's...different for you, ain't it?"

"It's okay, I won't be there too long, I'm sure. Just waiting for something better to come along. The wolf was at the door, as you used to say."

"Congrats. I gotta get up early myself so I'm going back to sleep now." He yawned for emphasis.

"Wait - how is he doing? Does he miss me?" Autumn pressed the phone closer to her mouth.

"I'm not doing this with you tonight. I gotta go."

"Okay, wait, I'm sorry. Just...just tell him I love him, okay? Can you do that for me please?"

Click.

Autumn sighed and laid the phone face down on the other pillow. At least this time, he didn't yell. In fact, he seemed pretty sweet and concerned about her well-being. Perhaps he was finally coming around to see things her way.

Another day, another dollar, Autumn sighed as she clocked in for her shift.

Her first month had gone by smoothly and Tony made it known that he was very proud of her inspection skills. None of her parts were rejected after clearing her station, and the workers at the assembly line fondly referred to her as Eagle Eye.

She grabbed another engine block casting off the conveyor belt, scrutinizing it carefully for any defects. Running her gloved fingers along the rough metal edges, she felt for any irregular bumps or scratches in the heavy steel chunk. This last station before quality testing was crucial. She had heard the horror stories of defective parts making it past the other inspectors and causing near-catastrophic failures after being installed. She took her job very seriously. The work may be a bit monotonous and tiring, but it allowed her to regain her independence and financial freedom, and it gave her a sense of pride to be responsible for something again.

As she turned the heavy casting over in her hands, a sharp sting bit into her pointer finger. Yelping in pain, she immediately dropped the part onto the table and the loud clanging it made as it struck the metal surface caused the other workers to swivel their heads in her direction. A thick thread of blood began pooling up from the deep cut. *Damn these cheap gloves*, she thought. The edges on that casting must have been extraordinarily sharp to slice through.

She used her teeth to pull off her other glove and hurried off toward the small first-aid alcove, blood dripping from her finger onto the concrete floor. The wound didn't seem too severe, but cuts anywhere were risky business around heavy machinery. A supervisor would need to record the incident before she could resume work.

Autumn located the well-stocked first aid kit on the wall and fumbled through bandages and ointments with one hand. The bleeding was slowing but the pain continued throbbing. She considered how easily a severed finger or lost limb could happen here, sending a chill down her back as she recalled the mystery of Sugar's missing finger.

"Autumn, what happened, are you okay?"

Victor stepped out of the glass office and stopped directly in front of her, cupping his hands beneath hers to gently grab her elbows.

Autumn stammered; his display of concern caught her off guard.

"How did this happen?" He looked into her eyes and behind his thick frames, she thought he looked worried.

"I don't know, just the edge of one of the parts, I didn't even see it!"

"This might scar, if we aren't careful. Here, let me help you," Victor said as he gently guided her over to the wash station. "I want to make sure it gets cleaned and bandaged properly."

He took the first aid kit from her hands and removed gauze pads and antiseptic wash. "This may sting a little bit," he warned as he began tenderly cleaning the cut to remove any dirt or debris. Victor was careful around the wound, moving with the skill and precision of an experienced medical technician. *Or, someone who had done this before.* Autumn reflected on the Days Without Incident sign and imagined someone had already reset it to zero, thanks to her.

Once it was cleaned, Victor noted that the bleeding had mostly stopped on its own. "I think you'll be okay now, you shouldn't need stitches," he assured her. He opened a small packet containing a finger bandage and carefully placed it over her cut, wrapping it snugly with the attached securing tape, giving the back of her hand an extra caress.

"There, is that feeling better?" he asked. "I know it still probably hurts, but keeping it covered will prevent infection and help it heal cleanly. Let me know if the bandage needs any adjusting or replacements. I'm right here if you need me."

"Wow, I don't know what to say - thank you, sir!" Autumn gazed into his eyes. What an extraordinary man. The care he had taken for her small wound melted her heart.

Victor closed up the first aid kit. "I'm so sorry this happened, Autumn. I know you're still new here, but your safety is important."

And with those final words, he disappeared behind the office door, leaving her alone with weakened knees, a properly bandaged finger, and damp panties.

She turned and headed back to her station, smiling softly to herself as she remembered the touch of his hands on her wrists. Sugar glared at her as she passed by her sorting station, and she flashed a big grin in return. The way Victor had just made her feel with the simplest effort, Sugar just might be in for a fight.

Two weeks had gone by and Autumn had not made any progress in her mission to capture Victor's heart. He seemed to be all business whenever she passed him on the floor. He had not so much as gazed into her eyes since the afternoon she cut her finger. But her desire for him had not faltered in the least. In fact, his disinterest only made her fire burn hotter.

Clad in the navy-blue uniform with the orange safety vest, she pulled her dark brown braids up into a bun and moved with practiced efficiency. She was careful to wear two pair of gloves this time but her eyes were keen, her fingers ran deftly over each component, ensuring smoothness in every detail. Yet, her thoughts were not solely occupied by the metal pieces before her; rather, they strayed sexy ass Victor making his daily rounds.

With his rugged charm and a no-nonsense demeanor, he walked the factory floor commanding respect from the workers. Autumn admired the way everyone paused when he approached, they wanted to greet him and spend just a moment in the warmth of his presence. His authority and competence sparked an attraction that seemed to blanket the entire room, men and women alike, their faces lit up when he came to their station.

Determined to catch his eye, Autumn adjusted her pace as he got closer, she hurried and checked the next three pieces in a row so that she would be free to chat without the line backing up. She felt him at her heel and she turned slowly with a ready grin - he simply nodded in her direction and kept walking to the next station.

Her heart dropped as she stared at his back.

He really just swerved me. She thought, incredulously.

This is what it feels like to be swerved. Wow.

The parts banging together on the belt shook her back to reality. She quickly shifted back to her work at hand and began angrily snatching the gears to the side.

"You mad?" Sugar yelled out from her table a few feet away.

Angrily, Autumn held up her middle finger and scowled. The other women at the table chuckled and shook their heads at the exchange. Feeling emboldened by their laughter, Autumn yelled back. "Mind your business!"

She stole a glance in Victor's direction but he seemed deeply engrossed in a conversation with one of the few male employees on the floor. They stood close, talking excitedly and pointing occasionally to the machinery around them. Undeterred, Autumn decided to take matters into her own hands. Picking up two of the door handles she had been inspecting, she walked purposefully towards Victor, her heart beating a little faster with each step.

"Hey, Victor," she greeted, a touch of nervousness in her voice. "I was wondering if you could take a look at these handles before I get too deep into the batch. They seem a little different than the last ones."

Victor's eyes briefly met hers, and he nodded, taking the parts from her hands. "Sure, Miss Lawrence, let me see." He rotated them and examined the edges, smoothing his finger across the surface. "Good idea to double check but these are fine," he acknowledged, shoving them back at her before returning his attention to the younger man.

Autumn refused to be disheartened. Her mind raced with thoughts of how to recapture the magic they'd shared two weeks earlier. Victor was attracted to her. He wanted her. Of that, she was certain. That sparkle in his eyes the day they met, that wasn't light reflecting off of the machinery. That was his true emotion shining through his soul, but since he was part owner of the family company, she understood that he couldn't risk it all by dating a subordinate. But there had to be something she could do to let him know that she was willing to be as flexible and discreet as he desired.

Perhaps a casual invitation to grab coffee on a weekend, or a shared moment discussing the intricacies of auto parts – anything to bridge the gap between their professional roles. He was trying extra hard to pretend like she meant nothing to him but she could see right through his charade.

She took the walk of shame back to her conveyor table and threw the handles on the roller bed. Her one-eyed coworker, Eve, affectionately known as Pirate, gave her a look of disapproval as she fumbled to catch up with the parts.

"What? What?" She demanded. Eve shook her head and continued working.

Suddenly, Autumn jammed her left hand between the rollers and held it there. The rollers pinched and crushed her fingers, as her hand swelled and the skin strained against the pressure. She bit her lip and fought back tears, staring defiantly across the tables at Sugar. Sugar stared back, her face a mixture of curiosity and shock, but a bit of a smile danced around the corners of her lips. Autumn felt her knees buckle, she used her free hand to balance herself on the edge of the table. The room began to spin in violent circles as intense pain shot up her arm and into her shoulder.

Eve finally sprang into action and slammed her hand on the safety stop button just beneath the table. The accident alarm sounded overhead and Autumn heard someone scream. The rollers opened and released her hand, allowing Autumn to tumble free in blessed relief from the agony. She felt someone embrace her from behind and gently guide her to the floor.

"I got you," Sugar's soft voice whispered into her ear as she bent her knees and lowered Autumn's head to rest.

In a daze of confusion and pain, Autumn spotted Victor rushing toward them; she felt him cradling her arm with his warm hands, heard him yelling in a panic, "Get some help over here!"

Could she be dreaming? Or was he really leaning over her, staring into her eyes with concern?

His face was close enough to hers that she only had to fight the pain, arch her back, and reach his lips-

"I think she's ready," said Victor, looking at Sugar.

He answered on the first ring this time. That was unusual, Autumn thought. *He must have been waiting for me to call.*

"What?"

"Um, hello?"

"What do you want, Autumn?" Instead of his normal patient tone, Geraldo was rude and clearly agitated.

"You're in a bad mood. I'll call you back."

"No - tell me what you want so you don't have to call back."

"Wow, okay then. So sorry for bothering you," Autumn felt defeated. Her hand throbbed horribly after the pain medication had worn off, and she just wanted to hear the sound of her son's voice.

"Why are you so mean?" She asked, fighting back tears.

The sound of rustling and movement filled her ear, followed by a woman's voice whispering in the background. *"Is that her again?"*

"WHO IS THAT?" screamed Autumn. "WHO DO YOU HAVE OVER THERE WITH OUR CHILD IN THE HOUSE?"

"Don't do this. Don't make *me* do this with you, Autumn," Geraldo responded in a measured tone. "I'll hang up right now and block you from calling."

"Wait - please don't hang up. I...I...I got hurt at work today. That's why I called," she calmed down, hoping he would give her another chance and continue the conversation.

"What happened? I heard bad things about that place but I didn't want to discourage you when you told me you were working there. I know you need this..."

"I crushed my hand. Pretty bad- "

Geraldo suddenly raised his voice, concerned. "Are you on something? Did they give you something for it?"

"Don't worry, they just gave me Tylenol 300. Nothing too heavy," Autumn paused. "They read my chart, I'm sure."

More rustling and mumbled voices in the background, as he covered the phone to speak to the woman in his house.

Autumn swallowed a lump in her throat. "Can I...can I talk to Brian? Please?"

"Have you been keeping up with your therapy? If you got hurt, you're supposed to report it - did you report it?"

"Not yet, I will tomorrow. Can I, please?"

"Bye, Autumn. And take your meds. Bye."

Click.

He was always the first to hang up. Even when she behaved.

And she always sat and stared at the phone in her hand for a little while after the called ended, as if he might just call back and apologize for his abruptness; claim that he didn't really mean to hang up on her. But he never called back.

She still had hope.

A text message popped up at the top of her phone screen and her heart gave a tiny leap.

Unknown number.

She tapped to open the message.

> Hey, it's sugar.

> Come meet me. I wanna show u sumtin.

Autumn hesitated, then remembered how kind Sugar had been during her crisis earlier that day. Her broken fingers - now wrapped and stented - still throbbed painfully, she couldn't text but she replied with a voice text.

> Meet where?

> 54892 west meadow drive

> I can't drive

> uber then

Were they friends now? She could use a friend. Maybe Sugar wasn't so bad after all. Or... maybe she'd seen how tenderly Victor handled her as she lay on the cold factory floor, and she was ready to concede the fight for his affection.

Autumn ordered an Uber and hurried to freshen up, excited for an opportunity to get to know Sugar outside of work, and make a real friend.

ele

West Meadow Drive was a beautiful name for a road in a particularly ugly part of town. At one point in time, perhaps the name was more fitting the neighborhood, but that would have been long before Autumn was born. Her entire life, that area was not the kind of place where you met up with coworkers for board games and charcuterie boards. The street unfolded with matching rows of small wood-framed homes, sitting on grass-bare lots of patchy dirt and crumbled driveways.

The Uber bumped along the rough pavement; the driver grunted each time he had to slow down significantly to crawl over a speed bump. Autumn could feel his frustration and made a mental note to tip him well for his trouble.

He pulled up to the address that Sugar supplied, as put into the app.

"This is it, ma'am," he said, looking at Autumn in the rearview mirror.

The front porch light was on but the rest of the small home looked to be dark inside. If it weren't for the multiple cars parked in the driveway and on the street directly in front, it might have appeared that no one was home.

Autumn rang the doorbell, waited for a few minutes and raised her hand to ring again when the door suddenly flew open and she found herself staring into Eve's big beautiful grin.

"Come on in, my dear - so happy you made it!" Eve exclaimed, taking Autumn's elbow to guide her inside. "How are you feeling?

Does this still hurt?" She asked, tapping gently on Autumn's injured hand.

Autumn didn't respond, she was focused on the sounds of voices rising from just beyond the foyer. Eve deftly slipped her purse from her good shoulder and dropped it on the entryway table, then waved Autumn to proceed into the living room.

To her surprise, there were at least 10 to 12 people in attendance; seated on the sofa, in the chairs, lounging on floor pillows or leaning against the wall. There were candles burning around the room, providing just enough light to illuminate their faces but making the experience a bit unsettling. In the middle of the room stood Sugar, dressed in a brightly flowered mumu; she was reading passages from a book held awkwardly between her 8 fingers.

When she spotted Autumn, she closed the book and seemingly breezed across the room to embrace her. Autumn was stiff in her arms, unsure and untrusting.

Sugar drew back and waved her arm around the room. "Relax, we're all family in here."

Autumn recognized the young man on the floor pillow whom Victor had been speaking with before her accident. Besides one other male standing in the doorway, the rest of the guests were the women who worked at Mayweather. Bobbette waved to her from the sofa, where she reclined with her broken foot propped up on the coffee table.

Seeing everyone together in one small room, away from the machinery and the obstruction of the conveyor tables, it was clear to Autumn for the first time that they were all injured or disabled in some manner. As she circled the room with her eyes, smiling and greeting each one, she realized that every person was wearing a bandage or a cast, an eye patch, an arm sling or a splint; there were even a few prosthetic arms and legs among the motley crew. They were all broken and patched back together.

My God. We're like the island of broken fucking toys in the hood. She thought to herself.

A girl she recognized from the original bathroom huddle suddenly squealed and began flapping the curtains. "He's here! He's here!" She rushed excitedly into the foyer, passing Autumn who noticed that she was barefoot and missing a middle toe on her right foot, causing her to skip lightly to avoid bearing weight on it. The others began to bustle around, straightening themselves - and each other - in anticipation of this guest of honor.

Sugar beamed in Autumn's face. "He's here!" She repeated, and danced away, leaving Autumn confused and unsure of what her role should be, as everyone else seemed already have assigned tasks and performances.

"Good evening, my precious beauties." Victor's silky bass floated into the room moments before he entered, bearing the biggest grin Autumn had ever seen on his face. Without his strict manager glasses, his intense brown eyes stood out even more in the dimly lit room, and his face was flush with excitement and desire. Casually dressed in a checkered-print button up shirt and slacks, he raised his arms out to the side and Sugar obediently began unbuttoning his shirt while Eve stepped in to work on the waistband of his pants.

Autumn was frozen into place, frightened but also weirdly aroused and fascinated. They swarmed Victor, working together to remove his clothing down to his boxers. They positioned their hands on his body and together pushed him down in the overstuffed chair.

She stumbled backwards as they jostled against her in their effort to form a single line in front of his throne. Autumn stared in amazement as they undressed and danced excitedly on their real and plastic feet, waiting their turn to approach Victor.

One by one, Victor gently caressed their broken parts, kissing the areas where the appendages were missing, licking the spots that were red, scarred and angry. His eyes rolled back in his head at the pleasure he was experiencing from blessing their afflictions. And the workers - they trembled in ecstasy as Victor's hands and lips patiently explored their bodies. Some had tears streaming down their cheeks, others rocked back and forth mumbling incoherent phrases like they were speaking in tongue.

Autumn was suddenly very afraid. This was the man she loved - at least, she thought she loved him - but this was too much freakiness even for her.

"I'm sorry, I can't," she muttered, grabbing her purse before darting out the door. She walked a few feet away from the house and pulled out her phone.

Crouching against the car parked in the driveway, Autumn fumbled with her phone in the dark. She laid it on the ground and tapped Geraldo's contact.

"You always answer, thank you for that," she breathed heavily into the phone.

"I'll always answer, you know that. I try, but I just want you to get better," he replied. "What's going on - you sound like you're running."

"I kinda got myself into a situation over here. Can you come get me?"

Silence.

"Please?" She begged.

"Autumn, I'm not alone right now. And I don't think that's a good idea anyway."

"Is she there again?"

Silence.

"She's my wife, Autumn. You know that. She lives here."

Autumn sobbed.

"Where are you? I can send you a cab or something. Or I can call your mom."

"I just wanna see Brian, just for a few minutes," Autumn cried. "I miss him so much."

"I know. I miss him too."

He listened to her cry for a few minutes and he didn't interrupt this time. He was good about that sometimes.

"I'm sorry."

"It wasn't your fault, Autumn."

"Do you think he knows that I'm sorry? Do you think he knows that I miss him?"

"He knows. And he wants you to be safe. Can you stay safe for him, and get better?"

Autumn nodded in the darkness, wiping her face and nose with the sleeve of her free arm. Her fingers tingled; the pain meds were beginning to wear off.

"I'm going to hang up now," she whispered, pushing against the car to raise up off the ground.

"Okay, take care of yourself," replied Geraldo.

This time, he waited for her to hang up first, and she did.

———*ℓℓ*———

When Autumn reentered the room, Victor had shed his boxers and was holding a fully naked Bobette on his lap. They were counting her fingers as she made fists and popped them up one by one like a child.

"Are you staying this time?" The one-eared woman from the bathroom was standing next to her holding a knife in one hand, covering her bloody breast with the other. Her eyes were glazed over and she wobbled from the pain, but her smile was as bright as the flames of the candles.

Autumn wanted that kind of peace and disconnect from reality; she wanted to experience that kind of freedom from the pain of her loss. She wanted what they shared. She started to undress and Bobette jumped up to assist her. When she was naked, she leaned toward Victor and stared into his eyes, begging him to let her into their secret club.

"You must do it yourself," he explained, taking the knife from the woman and placing it into Autumn's hand.

Autumn sank to the floor and began to count her toes with the tip of the knife.

Peace was near.

The Kids are Alright

We do things the old way.

Talia opened her eyes in darkness; groggy, her mouth sticky and sour. Her body felt as if she'd been hit by a bus and then dumped on the cot. Something warm spilled from between her legs when she pushed herself up to balance on her arms and try to make out the shapes of objects in the room. Next to the cot stood a cloth-covered table holding various bloodied utensils. She winced as she began to remember.

The sound of a baby crying in the distance jolted her out of the fog. Suddenly, she remembered.

Barefoot and clad only in a sheer gown, she dragged her aching body to the door and propelled herself down the hall toward the direction of the cries. Her head was spinning and she pressed her hands against the walls to steady herself

"Give me my baby, Auntie!" Talia held the knife out in front of her, but Auntie laughed, showing sharp teeth and flashing red pupils that were anything but joyous.

"No need for that, my love. Here you go." She pulled the flaps of the blanket over the distressed infant and handed her to her mother.

Talia turned to her son, seated on the stool against the wall.

"Get over here, Lowell! Get in front of me!"

The little boy jumped up and obediently positioned his small body in front of his mother, facing Auntie with as much of a scowl as an eight-year-old could muster.

"You don't know what you're doing, mi love." She said softly. "Your mother was wrong. Don't be like her."

Cradling her baby, Talia dropped to the floor and began chest compressions to force the water from her tiny lungs.

"You got to give her those claws now! Before this mean old world has a chance to hurt them!"

Baby Due began to cough and Talia quickly flipped her over to help clear her lungs. When the baby stopped choking and began to cry, Talia scooped her up in the blanket and jumped to her feet. She grabbed her son's shoulder with her free hand and began backing out of the room.

The woman folded her arms across her chest and watched her, smiling. "It is your child. Your wish. I'll be here when you need me," she said softly, as the pointed tips of her teeth slid back into her mouth.

"Thank you, but we'll be fine," Talia yelled over her shoulder as she pulled Lowell into the hallway. Her heart pounded in her chest and she struggled to breathe through the pain shooting through her body, but the front door loomed just a few feet ahead. She imagined her Auntie racing behind her to snatch her baby girl, but when her hand closed on the door handle, she exhaled in relief. Talia tumbled out onto the sidewalk gripping the baby in the crook of her arm and her son by the hand.

———elle———

Hey, hey, the kids are alright. Hey, the kids are alright.

It took everything in Talia to agree to Due attending an out-of-state college. She thought it best that her daughter remains closer to home, where Talia could better keep her safe from the unspeakable terrors of the world. But when Due earned a full ride to a major university over an hour away, Talia had no choice but to relent. The 18-year-old moved an hour away to live on campus, and for the first few months, she was by all accounts, happy and thriving. She began each day with a cheerful '*Good Morning, Mama*' text before heading off to her classes, and all seemed well, until one day, it wasn't. While Talia couldn't quite put her finger on it, she knew there was a problem bubbling beneath Due's happy exterior.

The problem's name was Robert.

Due revealed on her social media page the arrival of Robert into her life. After getting over the disappointment at not being invited into a more personal and intimate conversation about her first boyfriend, Talia pacified herself with browsing the happy selfies and photos of Due cuddled with her Robert, a round-headed rat-faced looking kid with oddly wide-spaced teeth. She decided that she didn't like him but she couldn't put her finger on the *why*.

Talia had spent so many years protecting Due from the world, but she had forgotten to prepare her for guys like Robert. For any guy, really. She'd repeated all of the mantras that her own mother had shared:

Men are dogs.

Men only want one thing.

Don't trust any man.

Attempting to instill a sense of dread and wariness that she felt would keep her out of the clutches of the worst kind of men. But she hadn't prepared her for Robert.

Talia sensed the change almost immediately.

The text messages became sporadic before stopping altogether; when Talia would call, the phone would ring several times before Due's trembling voice kicked in to announce her unavailability, but Talia's messages went unanswered. Even her social media presence had been reduced to bible passages and kitten memes, but nothing that offered a peek into what was going on inside of Due's world.

It was time to make an unannounced visit to the campus. Upon arrival, Due greeted her at the door with a look of confusion turning quickly into worry as she backed away from the door.

"What are you doing here, Mama?"

Talia wrapped her arms around the girl, marveling at how frail she was as her arms encircled the width of her body.

"Are you eating? You're so thin!" She exclaimed, pulling back to look into Due's face.

"I'm fine, Mama, stop." She shrugged out of Talia's tight embrace and adjusted her clothing; her sweatshirt hung limply on her frame as if it were at least two sizes too big. She kept her eyes down, addressing Talia and immediately looking away before making eye contact; something was indeed very wrong.

"I came up here to see what the hell is wrong with you. No calls? No texts? What's been going on?"

"Nothing's been going on; I've been busy with classes, finals and stuff. That's all."

"That's all? That's ALL? You drop out of touch for nearly three weeks and I'm supposed to just sit and wait until you find the time to reach out?"

Due turned her back and began moving about the tiny dorm room, straightening the pillows on her bed, dusting invisible specks from the bottles atop her dresser. She glanced back at Talia then stood gazing out of the window.

"Look at me, Due, turn around."

Due shrugged but didn't change her position, instead, she raised a hand and pretended to smooth wrinkles out of the curtain.

"DUE!" Talia grabbed the girl's shoulders and spun her around, zeroing in on what she'd missed when the door opened, what Due had so expertly hid by keeping her face aimed in the opposite direction: the remnants of a black eye.

Talia gasped and covered her mouth. "What happened to you – who did it?" Shocked, she whispered through her fingers.

"It was an accident, Mama, wait, don't get all crazy, he didn't mean it-"

"Where is he?" Talia placed her hands on her hips and demanded; Due attempted to dodge around her, but she planted her feet squarely in Due's path.

Due shrank, opening and closing her mouth but not saying a word.

"WHERE IS HE?" Talia repeated, louder this time. "You know I will knock on every door in this building until I find him. Is that what you want?"

Slowly, Due raised her arm and pointed, whispering, "122."

Talia spun on her heel and abruptly left the dorm room to charge down the hallway. She read the numbers on the doors as she passed, stopping when she reached the door with 122 stenciled across the panel. Using her fists to announce her visit, she realized the door was steel, and it made her even angrier as she imagined Due cowering in her own room while Robert attempted to kick his way inside.

"Open the door, Robert. I wanna talk to you!" Talia pounded on the door again. When the knob turned and the door pulled inward, she quickly jammed the point of her boot into the crack and pushed forward with the weight of her body. She paused a moment to consider the frightened young man bracing the wall directly behind the door; scanning his face, she determined that he couldn't possibly be Robert. But the figure standing two feet away fumbling with his cellphone - she supposed he was making an effort to summon help – *that* would be Robert. She recognized him from the photos Due posted during happier days, but at that moment, he looked the exact opposite of the boy who made Due smile.

She crossed the room in two great strides and knocked the phone from his hands; it smashed against the brick wall and fell to pieces on the carpet.

"Hey-" Robert opened his mouth to protest when Talia grabbed his throat with both of her hands, forcing him backwards until she slammed him against the window pane.

"Do you wanna die?" She asked him through clenched teeth.

He couldn't answer, her grip was too tight; she squeezed tighter.

"You must want to die because you gave my daughter a black eye and that's the behavior of someone who wants to die."

He raised his arms and attempted to break her hold, but his efforts were useless in the face of such rage. She moved one hand from his throat and swatted his arms away with a chuckle. Her free hand dropped to his crotch where she gripped his package and locked in tightly, squeezing until Robert's body crumpled. She released him and let him fall at her feet, crying and cupping between his legs.

"Aw, this was just a tickle. If I have to come back, it's going to really hurt," she spat at him, delivering a hard kick into his shoulder.

—*ell*—

That was the last she'd heard or seen of Robert, and Due enjoyed her remaining college years in peace. Shortly after graduation, she began a career in social work and settled into her new life across the country. Talia was comforted by their weekly phone calls, and she was amused at Due's journey into adulthood.

But when she arrived home unannounced that Saturday morning, Talia felt uneasiness building in the pit of her stomach.

Due stood on the doorstep with a big wide grin, and she fell forward into her mother's arms as soon as the door opened. Talia hugged her tightly, burying her face in her braids and saying a silent prayer that her daughter was safely home.

The young man standing directly behind them cleared his throat and Talia let go of her daughter and smiled.

"Oh, I'm sorry, you're the driver – how much was it? Due baby, you need money?"

Due slipped her hand into his and they stood on the porch beaming at Talia; her heart dropped.

"Mama, this is Kevontae, but you can call him YTK KEV," Due flashed the brightest smile that Talia had ever seen on her face.

Talia paused, collecting herself before she spoke and extended her hand.

"Nice to meet you, YTK Kev."

"What's up?" He returned a limp non-impressive shake with only fingers.

"Kev is a rapper!" Due exclaimed, clapping her hands excitedly. "He's going to do a show in Seattle, so I'm going to stay here with you and he can pick me up on the way back. Right, Kev?"

"Yup," YTK Kev had already turned his attention to his vibrating phone.

Talia sized him up as they made their way into the house and settled in the living room. He was attractive, dressed like a lot of the so-called rappers she had seen on television, saggy jeans, boots, leather jacket, with a spread of random tattoos spilling from the neckline of his t-shirt and covering his throat. Smooth brown skin, pierced ears, curly Mohawk, he had covered all of the items on the Beginning Rapper Checklist. He looked like trouble, Talia thought to herself as she bustled around the kitchen preparing snacks and drinks.

Due spun around the living room like a child at Christmas, chattering excitedly to YTK Kev as she pointed to the family photos covering the walls. She finally took a breath and strained her head toward the hallway. "Is Lowell here too? I want him to meet Kev!"

"How about we sit down first so you can tell me more about this thing you're going to see." Talia sat on the sofa and waved her hand for the young couple to join her.

"Mama, this music festival is really huge! So many big names are gonna be there and Kev might end up signing with one of the majors – right, honey?"

YTK Kev continued replying to what sounded like a flurry of text messages, looking up briefly to nod.

"Well, that sure sounds exciting. Congratulations. That's got to mean a lot of big changes in your life, right?" Talia returned to the room with a pitcher of lemonade and three glasses, setting the tray in front of the couple.

YTK Kev shrugged. "I guess, it'll be cool. I'll be doing a lot more shows, that's one thing."

"Rap one of your songs, baby! Mama, listen to this!"

On cue, Kev began bobbing his head and gesturing with his hands as he rapped some words about being some kind of shark. Or maybe it was about being on Shark Tank, Talia couldn't tell, but it didn't sound too bed if she were forced to admit. Still, something about him raised the hairs on the back of her neck and her instincts were never wrong.

Talia watched as Due jumped into action. She poured Kev's glass first, her hands shook slightly as she handed it to him, spilling the liquid over the sides.

YTK Kev sighed and shook his head, clearly irritated with her service. Talia bristled as she watched their interaction.

His phone buzzed again and he looked at the screen then stood to leave.

"Well, I better get going. Still have a ways to drive," he said, heading for the door.

"Wait, baby!" Due jumped up and ran behind him, throwing her arms around his waist just as he reached the door. "Kiss me goodbye!" She squealed.

He turned and offered a slight peck on the cheek before slipping out the door, leaving Due standing in the doorway.

Talia attempted to fill the awkward space with some words of comfort.

"Baby, come help me finish this coffee cake!"

Due smiled but her eyes didn't. "Mama, I want wine."

"Then wine you shall have!"

Minutes later, the two women chatted enthusiastically over buttery bites of coffee cake.

"I think this is really *it*." Due murmured. Cinnamon crumbs tumbled down her chin and onto the front of her blouse; Talia wrestled with the urge to reach out and flick them away, so she just stared as they collected inside of the fold at the buttons.

Due continued on without encouragement.

"See, I already know what you're thinking, Mama, but this time is different. It's really different. You gotta trust me, for real."

Trust me, Talia thought wryly. S*aid the spider to the fly.* YTK Kev was the spider and Due just a fly struggling in his web.

Due's shoulders danced as she ate heartedly and sipped from the glass of wine Talia had poured. The evening sun slipped through the drawn blinds and bathed her kinky twists in gold, and Talia thought her daughter had never looked more joyful. Her eyes twinkled as she prattled on about her plans with Kevontae aka YTK Kev.

Due reached across the table and covered Talia's hand with her own. "Don't worry so much. I'm really okay this time. God sent Kev to me."

Talia took a deep drag from her cigarette while regarding her daughter with narrowed eyes. "You sure about that?"

"Yes. Yes." Due paused, then said again, emphatically. "Yes, I'm certain this time."

Talia extinguished the cigarette into the ashtray on the table, pressing down until the red embers turned black and sent a thin plume of smoke into the air.

"I'll run you a nice bath and then you can get in the bed and rest up for your trip tomorrow." Without waiting for confirmation, she pushed herself up from the table and headed up the stairs. Moments later, there was the familiar squeal of faucet knobs and the sound of rushing water filling the tub. The scent of lavender soon came floating down the stairs as Talia sprinkled bath salts into the hot water.

Due made her way toward the bathroom and found her mother standing in front of the mirror, gazing sadly at her own reflection. She stepped behind her, placing a hand on one shoulder and resting her head on the other. Their eyes met in the glass and Talia forced a smile, although the quivering of her lips belied the spark in her eyes. They shared a moment of undeniable love before Talia broke their embrace by ducking behind her daughter to catch the tub from overflowing.

"All ready, baby girl - let me help you," Talia reached for the hem of Due's tee shirt, pulling the fabric over her head and arms. Her eyes fell upon an angry dark bruise in the center of Due's chest and she gasped. A misshapen patch of broken blood vessels approximately the size of a fist; the trauma appeared to be at least two weeks old, the edges faded toward the center but it still looked painful and the intentional.

"Um, mom, help?" Due wiggled her arms, captive inside of the shirt covering her head.

Talia cleared her throat and helped Due free her arms. Turning her back to step out of her jeans, she revealed a similar purplish bruise along the side of her thigh. Talia offered her arm for balance, helping the girl step into the tub and ease her body beneath the bubbles.

Talia swallowed hard and kneeled at the back of the tub, using the sponge to scoop soapy water onto her daughter's back. Due drew her knees up to her chest and rested her head.

"I didn't realize I was so sleepy. I could fall asleep right now," she mumbled, leaning back against the tub.

Talia removed the big plastic clip from her head and let her braids fall down the side of the tub. She ran her fingers through the braids, lightly massaging her scalp; her fingers fell upon a bald patch that had scabbed over. She parted the braids and peered closely. "What happened here?"

Due squirmed away, reaching up and pull her braids over her shoulder and hide the bad patch from her mother.

"It got snatched out; it'll grow back."

"Snatched...snatched out?"

"Caught in the car door, it's okay, it'll grow back."

"Caught in the...car door, huh?"

Due shrugged and sank down into the tub until the water line was just below her collarbone. "I'm really sleepy, Mom. I think I might fall asleep right here. So sleepy," she murmured, her voice trailing off as her body relaxed.

Talia choked back tears as one tumbled down her cheek landing on top of the scab in her daughter's scalp. Due's shoulders slumped and her words faded to an incoherent mumble as the crushed Xanax in the wine took effect. Talia swallowed hard and gripped Due's shoulders firmly, pushing her beneath the soapy water until her fingers touched the bottom of the tub.

Under the influence of the drug, Due struggled weakly against Talia's arms holding her down. Her eyes popped open in fear and bubbles rose to the surface when she opened her mouth to scream. Talia almost faltered in that moment as her eyes met Due's and she saw the fear in her daughter's eyes as she fought the water rushing into her nostrils and into the scream of her open mouth. Her eyes were accusing, angry, afraid, confused. Talia squeezed her eyes shut and continued to hold the girl under the water. Due thrashed, kicking her legs against the bottom of the tub in an effort to push herself upward against Talia's force. She took her own arms and whipped them backward, scratching at her mother's forearms in an attempt to free herself.

As she tore at the skin of Talia's arm, she revealed the shiny red flesh beneath her human skin, and it was angry and raw and sinewy, but it did not bleed and Talia did not blink nor loosen her grip. She knew that if she softened just a bit, if she gave any opening for Due to break free, it would be over and she would never get another opportunity. In fact, if she failed at this moment, she would never get another chance to do anything else.

Talia felt a shift in the water, and felt the body beneath her fingers begin to change.

After a few moments, Due's arms went limp and dropped into the water as she gave up.

A vintage analog clock hung on the wall next to the bathroom mirror; in the silence, the sound of the second-hand ticking was as loud as a grenade as it moved around the dial.

Shaking, Talia pulled herself up to sit on the edge of the tub. Keeping her eyes on her daughter's body beneath the water, she counted softly to herself at the beat of the second-hand. She knew how long it should take. If she did it correctly.

Ten. Nine. Eight...

Three. Two. One.

Waiting.

Too long.

Then...bubbles.

Due's eyes opened as she surged out of the tub encased in a tidal wave of bath water. A series of growls erupted from her throat, at first low and unsure, until it rumbled, loud, intentional, bouncing off the walls of the bathroom and stirring the air.

Talia quickly snatched a large towel from the bar, throwing it across the girl's shoulders and lifting her out of the tub. She helped her stand on shaky legs before pulling her into an embrace; Due's body stiffened but after a moment or two, she relaxed and wrapped herself into the warmth of Talia's body. Silently, they held onto each other, until

Talia felt the shifting of bone beneath the towel.

Talia hugged her legs against her chest and rocked softly back and forth. The sun was going down and the evening chill cut straight through her gown and into her bones.

Lowell returned with her cherished quilt throw blanket that she kept at the foot of her bed, the one she'd always fussed about no one borrowing or even touching. Her own mother had taken her final sleep wrapped up in that blanket so it was both fitting and touching that Lowell had unwittingly selected it to bring her warmth. He draped it across her shoulders and tucked the ends beneath her hips to block out the cold air.

"Help me lie down, baby," she whispered, her breath forming tiny white clouds that hung in the air and then collapsed to the porch and shattered like ice.

Once positioned on her side in a fetal position, she closed her eyes and relaxed as her body weakened. She wasn't afraid of the process. Before she assisted in her mom's transition, she'd helped her sister, an aunt and even a couple of neighbors. But she had allowed herself to get a little too comfortable in this human shell, when all along it was clear that Due needed to be released sooner than later.

She twisted her head weakly toward the wet noisy sounds of slurping, chewing and grunting coming from the grassy area at the bottom of the steps. Due was making quite a mess of Kevontae's corpse as she ate with wild abandon. Unrecognizable while she fed, a fine layer of silky fur covered her body and her spine curved at an obscene angle as she bent over to ravage the corpse. Long talons sprung from her fingertips, certainly handy for ripping the flesh from her lover's bones yet daintily swiping the bits between her sharp teeth.

And yet, she's still so lovely. Talia thought as she watched her daughter with pride.

Lowell patted her shoulder through the blanket. "I think she's gonna be okay, Ma. You can go now."

"Watch out for her, Lo."

Due slowed down and settled back on her legs, resting, burping; her body began the transformation back to her human skin but the beast would always be just beneath the surface, waiting, watching, listening for its name to be called.

Lowell laughed. "She gotta watch out for me!"

The kids were gonna be alright. Talia smiled and went toward sleep.

B.M.G.

DODGE MILLER WAS HIS name; dropping bodies was his game.

Dodge chuckled at his own wit as he entered Daddy's bar and looked around for an empty seat. He settled onto a stool at the furthest end of the long counter, near the quieter side of the open dining room. He wanted peace, whiskey and french fries so he could think and strategize. The sign out front beckoned to him, Daddy's Place to Eat, Talk, Drink Coffee and Shit. He needed to do all of that, except talk, he didn't want to talk to anyone until he could figure out his next move.

It had been a no good very bad day. Nothing had gone according to plan and you know what they say about plans. He missed his mark and now he couldn't go home because...well...it might get ugly. As someone who usually made things ugly for others, he shuddered to think of what that meant for him.

He ordered some coffee with a Jack Daniels shooter and a chicken dinner platter, then began swiping through his phone for a place to sleep tonight.

A man dropped down two stools over and he bristled, pulling his jacket snug to conceal the gun stuck in his waistband.

"All these stools here and you gotta sit next to me?" Dodge growled at the intrusion.

The man grunted a reply as he focused on positioning his heavy rolling case beneath the counter. He pushed it in tight, as if he were afraid that someone might come along and swipe it right from between his legs.

"Traveling?" Dodge asked next, nodding his head toward the suitcase at the man's foot. He didn't want company but something about this guy was intriguing.

The man grunted again and waved at the server.

"Yeah, a little bit."

Dodge sipped his coffee for a few minutes, but out of the corner of his eye, he could see the man was patting the case at his knee. He had to know the story. Besides, it might be a good distraction from his own troubles.

"Where you from?" Dodge asked. "I don't know this area myself, just passing through. Trying to figure out how best to get back out."

"Not too far, either way, just keep going about 5 miles and you'll see the freeway to take you North or South. People get stuck at Daddy's all the time, something about it."

"Must be the sign," Dodge laughed and plucked a matchbook from the tray on the bar with Daddy's coffee pot logo stamped on the front flap. "Not too many places offer you a place to shit, in bright lights," He tapped his finger on the matchbook.

"What? Oh, yeah," The man joined him in laughter. "Well, to be fair, it's not really advertising a place to shit. What he meant was, you can do all kinds of shit here, but the way the sign turned out... He just rolled with it. Funny as hell though."

He leaned over and offered his hand. "I'm Will. Been coming here since I was a kid."

"Nice to meet you, Will. Dodge Miller." As he leaned across the stool to shake hands, he noticed Will bump the case with his knee. As someone who'd had his share of strange things inside of cases, he was really curious to see if Will might show him something he'd never seen before.

"You come here a lot, what's up - don't like the wife's cooking?" He nodded toward the wedding band on Will's ring finger.

Seemingly embarrassed, Will slipped the ring off his finger and dropped it into his jacket pocket. "Thanks for reminding me that I no longer have a wife. I meant to take that off a few days ago."

"Ouch. That new?" Dodge replied, feeling that he was just scratching the surface.

Will drained his coffee cup and signaled for a refill. "You ever wish you could turn back time? Like, squeeze your eyes shut and wish really hard, but every time you open them, shit is still fucked up?"

"Sounds like what I was doing before you sat down here," Dodge joked.

"Well, you know just what I mean then. But I bet you never ruined your whole life in 72 hours."

"I'm all ears. I got nowhere to go but back on that long dark road," Dodge reached into his pocket and pulled out a flask; he poured a little into his fresh cup of coffee and offered it to Will before he began his tale.

"She's coming!"

"What?"

Will raised his head briefly to throw a look of interest toward his wife, before returning his eyes to the naked bodies on his laptop display.

"She's coming. I got an email. She's really coming this time."

He used his fingertip to navigate through a few more screens of debauchery then sighed and double-tapped to close the browser window.

"*Who* are we talking about, honey," Both elbows now on the dining table and chin in hand, Will faced his wife. Sunny's distress was as evident on her face as it was in her voice. Her hands paused on the sides of her untouched plate as she met Will's eyes. She held her bottom lip between her teeth, eyebrows crinkled with worry.

"Michelle. She'll be here tomorrow."

"Michelle?"

"My sister, Will. Fuck's sake, do you seriously not know the names of my family members after being married for six freaking years?" She brushed her hand at the tear cascading down her cheek.

"I'm sorry, babe. Of course, I remember, I didn't hear what you said at first. I thought you said Rochelle - you know, your friend from up North."

"I haven't mentioned Rochelle since the wedding! Why would I suddenly announce that *Rochelle* was coming? Huh?"

"Well, you haven't mentioned Michelle in a while either - what made her pop up today?"

"I don't know. I don't know," Sunny shook her head. "I just opened my email and there it was."

She slid her cellphone across the table. "Look at it, just open it and read it. She does this shit to me."

Will pressed the button on her phone and paused at the lock screen. "Passcode?"

Sunny sighed and took the phone out of his hand, tapping the screen to grant him access.

"When did you lock it?" He asked when she returned the phone to his hand.

"I don't know, remember I got a new phone and just never removed the pin," Sunny shrugged.

"Ah, here it is," exclaimed Will as he opened the email containing Michelle's name. "Hmm, yeah, I see. She didn't say much, did she? She misses you, wants to see you, is leaving her husband - wait, when did she get married?"

Sunny sighed and held out her hand for the phone. "Last year, Will. She got married last year. I told you; her wedding was the same weekend I had to go away for the leadership conference and you stayed home with the boys."

"I don't remember any of that; I can't believe you missed your sister's wedding."

"I didn't have a choice! It was so last minute! It's not like they planned this big elaborate event, it was damn near a shotgun wedding. I couldn't get out of my conference without a damn good reason."

"It helps that you hate her guts, I mean, that makes it easier to miss stuff like that."

"I do NOT *hate* her. We just have a complicated relationship," Sunny read the email again, her forehead creased with worry.

Will reached for her forearm and gently stretched it out, turning it over to look at the deep, angry welt that remained from the stitched wound. He fingered the ragged copper edges and raised his eyes to meet hers.

"Looks like at least one time when she didn't agree with you right here."

Sunny snatched her arm away and pushed from the table.

"That was a long time ago. We've moved beyond that. She was out of control and off her meds."

The spot began to itch and she rubbed it against her hip. It always itched when she thought of Michelle, almost as if it remembered its origin. Of course, that was silly - but that's how it felt.

She didn't think of her often. They'd mostly avoided each other in all form unless it was a family event Sunny could not conjure up a powerful enough excuse to decline. Like their maternal grandmother's funeral two years prior. They exchanged awkward hugs at the casket as they passed with the rest of the family and Sunny felt Michelle linger a bit too long during the pull back. She didn't want to think too deeply into it, but it played over and over in her mind for months after.

Was that supposed to be their moment to bury the past? Forgive and forget? But how do you forgive someone who tried to kill you?

—*ell*—

A few days passed by, and then she was there.

Will looked up from his keyboard and blinked his tired eyes, and when he opened them again, there she was.

He hadn't laid eyes on her since the wedding. Back then, she was all legs and arms, with the slim, toned body of an athlete. She was cute like Sunny, her sister, but more of a tomboy and nothing he'd ordinarily look at longer than a minute or two.

The woman who walked in the door that day was really something else. No longer little Michelle in a baseball cap, this Michelle was a grown woman who had filled out quite nicely in all of the right places. He didn't know if it was all natural or if she had surgical help, but she had hips and thighs and lips and a waist that women were paying good money for.

The way she floated in and made a bee-line to pull Will into an embrace, a little voice in the back of his head yelled DANGER! DANGER! BACK UP RIGHT NOW! But what could be the harm? After all, her sister was now his sister too, right?

Later, when he recalled that first day she arrived, he would swear that sunlight flooded the hallway behind her body and a choir started singing somewhere in the distance. In his mind, she didn't just walk into the house, it was more like the house opened up for her presence, and something in his gut told him right then that he needed to get on the phone and schedule some work out of town or any excuse to get the hell out of the house for a few days.

And the flirting! If he and Sunny were in a discussion about something as mundane as paint samples, Michelle would chime in to take whichever side Will was on, even if her sister had the better position. It was clear that she wanted Will's attention and favor, but Sunny chalked up to her sister's sexually aggressive behavior to Michelle being resentful of the years they'd spent apart. She didn't want to speak on it and cause trouble that would force her sister out of her life again.

So, for his wife, Will endured the temptation, because tempting it was. She came at him from every turn and his body reacted in ways of which his mind was deeply ashamed. Michelle was incredibly sensuous and her signature perfume had strong notes of jasmine – he knew because it was the same scent that Sunny wore and she often talked about how the smell of jasmine made her feel sexy no matter what she wore.

With each day that passed, Will was more and more uncomfortable with Michelle staying in their home. But her visit did not have an end date, and he wasn't sure how to approach the discussion with his wife.

"Hey, I know you've missed your only sister all of these years but when do you think she'll be getting the fuck out of here?"

He just focused on staying out of the way, but the house wasn't big enough for the three of them. And sure enough, the trouble started the first time Sunny left the two of them home alone.

Each Wednesday, Sunny traveled to the Farmer's Market with friends, and although the market only ran until 3, the women routinely turned it into an entire day of shopping and drinks. Sunny eagerly invited her sister to join them, but Michelle declined, insisting she was looking forward to resting from her travels.

Less than ten minutes after Sunny pulled out of the driveway, Michelle made her first move. Working in his office, the sounds of the house drowned out by the noise of Will's furious typing on the keyboard. Suddenly, Will felt hands caressing the back of his neck.

He jumped up and out of his chair, knocking the keyboard tray loose from the desktop where it clattered noisily to the floor.

"WHAT THE FUCK, MICHELLE!!" Angry, he tried to back away but she had him cornered in the very center of the L-shaped desk. She moved in, pressing her body against his until their foreheads touched. Will turned his head to the side and she locked her lips into the flesh of his neck, sucking and pulling furiously. He tried to push her off of him but she gripped his neck even tighter. He was dismayed at the thought of the hickey she was surely leaving in her wake, but he was even more distraught at the way his dick was rising up in excitement as she pressed her hips against his.

Her lips made a wet sucking sound when she finally let go of his throat; he was helpless as she continued grinding her pelvis against him and deftly unzipped his pants and removed his dick with one hand.

<hr />

"Wait, hold on," Dodge interrupted him. "Your sister-in-law wants to fuck and you don't wanna mess up your happy home - just kick her sneaky ass out. Tell your wife what she's up to and kick her out! What am I missing here?"

Will took a long swig from his glass and sat it back down on the counter.

"You're missing that it wasn't that easy. You think if it was that easy, I'd be here today? With this?" He kicked the case with his foot, and Dodge swore that he heard a thump in reply, but he told himself it was just the liquor kicking in.

"Nah, man," Will continued. "The more I tried to resist, the harder she came after me."

"You never had to turn down pussy? It's hard, but it's not that hard."

"She wasn't taking no for an answer, or she was going to take the whole house down with her. And you might not believe this, but whenever she got on me, I felt like...you ever see those nature shows and the insect is stuck in the web and can't move, literally CANNOT move? That's how I felt every time she attacked me." Will sighed deeply and Dodge wanted to laugh but he could see the man's tortured face in the mirror behind the counter.

The waitress arrived with another round of drinks and a refill of fries for Dodge. Will reached up to accept the glass and his sleeve pulled back, exposing a dark irregular tattoo etched into his left wrist. Dodge leaned closer to read it in the dim light.

"BMG? What's that? Your nickname or something?"

Will chuckled and used his forefinger to smudge the ink. "It's not real, see? Bitch must go." He smirked and added. "Manifestation and all that shit."

"Did it work?" asked Dodge, genuinely curious.

"Well, let me finish my story."

As if their unintentional affair wasn't bad enough, Michelle took every opportunity to taunt him about their secret. She would stand behind Sunny and wink at him over her shoulder, or even open her robe and flash him, darting quickly away before Sunny could turn around. Will wanted to dig a hole in the backyard, crawl into it and die in peace. But a part of him was afraid that Michelle would crawl into the hole and start humping him as the life drained from his body into the soil.

She was impossible to avoid, impossible to resist, and apparently, impossible to get rid of, as Sunny was now suggesting that she might stay the entire summer as she waited for the proceeds from her divorce to come in. Will had been reduced to merely her sex slave, a prisoner in his own home. There would be no escape unless he came clean with Sunny and enlisted her help to get rid of her sister, after which they'd most likely divorce. He would be free, but at her expense, and he would die before he let Sunny feel the pain from his betrayal.

But how long must he suffer?

There was truly only one way out.

—ele—

The first time he killed her, she'd just finished riding him for 45 solid minutes until she began screaming and whipping her head from side to side, shuddering. Her face was contorted into a frightening mask behind which her eyes glowed a fiery red. It was over in a flash and her beautiful features returned in the blink of an eye. He lay there drained and confused, convincing himself that the transformation was just his mind playing tricks on him as she sucked every bit of semen from his tender nuts. His body performed but his head was busy plotting how to end the misery. She had her leg thrown across his waist trying to snuggle as if they were passionate lovers; while

Will tried to figure out how he kept ending up beneath her when each time he vowed it would never happen again.

"We have to stop this," he finally gathered enough strength to whisper, afraid of how she would react.

Just as he feared, she immediately straddled him and leaned over into his face.

"Why?" She demanded.

"Because it's not right and you know it. I don't want to hurt Sunny," he said softly, choosing his words carefully.

Michelle laughed so hard that he could feel her stomach rippling against his.

"Sunny doesn't care. You think she cares? Ha! You're such a fool," she spat in his face. "Where do you think your sweet Sunny is right now? Huh?"

Will tried to push her off of him but the weight of her body was incredibly heavy and his mind couldn't comprehend in that moment *why*. He pushed against her shoulder futilely but he couldn't move her.

"She's doing the same thing we just did, but with someone bigger and harder and better than you!" Michelle grinned in his face and her mouth stretched wide enough to swallow his entire head.

He was terrified. The words coming out of her mouth didn't matter, he was scared of *her* or *it* or whatever she was in that moment. He screamed and used all of his strength to bolt up from the bed, knocking her over the edge of the bed where she hit the floor. She continued to laugh and scream at him.

"You fool! Sunny isn't worried about you!"

The garage door began sliding open and Will's heart dropped. He guessed that Sunny had already hit the opener as soon as she turned onto the street, so there were about 4 more minutes before she'd be walking up the stairs to the bedroom. There was no time to explain or reason, he had to act quickly.

He dived over the bed and wrapped his hands around Michelle's throat to stop her from laughing. He squeezed and squeezed until his fingers touched; the laughter stopped but that grin – that grin was still on her face.

Even after the light in her eyes turned off and her body went limp. She kept grinning.

Will heard the car door slam and he estimated the amount of time he needed to hide Michelle's body until he could make up a story and dispose of it later. He dragged her down the hall and pushed her into the closet of the empty bedroom they were saving for their first baby. They rarely even looked in there anymore so that should buy him a few hours.

With Michelle securely tucked away beneath a pile of blankets, Will jumped in the shower to freshen up before greeting Sunny. They met on the stairs and he attempted to hug and kiss her cheek but she pulled away and said, "Ugh, honey, not right now, I'm hot and sweaty, let me shower first – meet you in the kitchen!" He watched her back in amazement as she skipped down the hallway, past the baby's room, and disappeared into their bathroom.

Michelle's last words rang in his ear, but she was just trying to get inside of his head, right? What would she know about Sunny? They didn't even like each other!

Will headed to the kitchen and fixed himself a sandwich, humming softly as he contemplated how he would finish the task at –

He heard voices upstairs, Sunny was laughing and talking loudly with...Michelle. A piece of bread lodged in his throat when she and Michelle walked into the kitchen together. Sunny, freshly showered with her damp hair pulled up into a bun, and Michelle looking just as fresh and bright, wearing the same lounging set she wore when he wrapped his hands around her throat just minutes earlier.

———*ele*———

"What do you mean you killed her? You must not have choked hard enough!" Dodge was in disbelief at this part of the story. And as someone who had choked a lot of bitches in his line of work, he knew that if you did it right, they didn't get back up.

"She was dead, man. Granted, I haven't seen a lot of dead people up close in my life-time, but I know what dead looks like. She was gone," Will said, shaking his head.

"Well, I HAVE seen a lot of dead people in my line of work – and that bitch wasn't dead. No way. Unless you wanna tell me she turned into a zombie or some shit!"

The men paused their conversation as the server appeared again to remove their plates and wipe the counter.

"Can I get you guys something else?" She asked.

"Nothing thanks!" Dodge replied quick-ly, anxious to get back to Will's story. Hours later he had been annoyed at the strange man sitting too close to him, but now he was pleased to be a part of this wild ride that Will was taking him on. He needed to hear the rest, especially the part leading up to whatever was in the suitcase.

"Alright, what happened next? Did you fuck her again?" He asked Will, excitedly.

"Naw, no more of that. From that point on, it was war - Operation BMG," Will tapped the letters inked onto his wrist and continued his story.

* * *

Later that same evening of Michelle's resurrection, Will pulled out Sunny's family photo albums, hoping to learn something about her and Michelle's life together. Sunny walked into the room as he sat on the bed examining the photos.

"What you doing, hon? Going down *my* memory lane?" She dropped onto the bed next to him and gently took the album from his hands. Sunny flipped the plastic covered pages, stopping briefly on each page to sigh wistfully and run her hand across the film. Will felt a little ashamed that he had never paid much attention to the evidence of his wife's childhood. He'd listened to her narrate her life over the years but in this moment, it was very clear that he hadn't paid any attention.

As she flipped through the photos of high school, he noticed for the first time that Michelle was missing from most if not all of the scenes.

"You and Michelle are only a couple years apart – why isn't she in any of these? Did she go to a different high school?"

Sunny looked at him and frowned. "Okay, now I know I told you about her sickness when we were teens."

"Sick?"

She sighed and shook her head like he was an annoying child.

"She got really sick when she was 12. She started complaining about feeling too weak to get up out of bed for school. This went on for a while until my parents took her to the doctor and found out she had leukemia."

"Oh man, that's awful," Will immediately felt nauseous. All of the horrible thoughts he'd had about her, suddenly felt unwarranted despite the hell she had been putting him through behind Sunny's back.

"Yeah, treatment was pretty brutal, many times we didn't think she'd even wake up. And at one point..." Sunny's voice trailed off and she dropped her eyes.

"At one point?"

"We almost did lose her. I mean, the machines stopped beeping and she did that long sound where a person's heart stops. Then they revived her and she started gasping for air."

"You were there?"

Sunny nodded. "We all were around her bed because they told us she wouldn't make it through the night."

"Anyway, she had to be in therapy for a long time, but she eventually got better. I think that's when she changed. I think that's when she got meaner."

Will felt a shiver run up his spine as he remembered Michelle's face hovering above his, her nostrils flared and the pupils of her eyes ablaze.

"It's almost like she resented me for not being sick. She would just sit around and stare at me with all of this hate in her eyes," Sunny continued. "She would refer to herself as the dead bitch, if she got upset about something, she'd say, "oh sure, blame it on the dead bitch."

"My God," Will exclaimed softly.

They sat quietly just looking at the photos until Will spoke again.

"But when she came to the wedding, you said you hadn't seen each other since you were 15 – did she get sick again?"

Sunny shook her head. "We had to send her away again. She came into my room one night and held a pillow over my face until my mom heard me kicking the wall and she stopped her."

Will lightly touched the bruise on her arm. "This?"

She nodded. "I seemed to have a lot of accidents after she came back from the dead!" Sunny rolled her eyes, while forming air quotes with her fingers.

The second time he killed her - or at least, tried to kill her - he approached the task with a bit more motivation, frustration and anger. It had been two weeks since he first failed at ending their twisted relationship and she was revving up to climb his bones again. As long as she was in the house, Will tried to stay in the open spaces, close to Sunny whenever possible, but Sunny had her own reasons for leaving the house and she didn't seem to notice or care about Will's obvious discomfort around her sister. He tried to get her to cancel her market trip the next week, offered to take her to dinner and a movie, but she insisted the girls would be so disappointed if she backed out.

After Sunny left for the day, Will slipped into the mud room to get his laundry from the dryer, in hopes of escaping the house himself. Michelle caught him in the laundry room and slammed against his back with all of her force.

"Hey baby, I've missed you," she growled into his ear from behind. She pressed her breasts into his back and reached around to his crotch area.

"NO!" He tried to shrug her off but she locked her arms around him tightly and he was amazed again at how incredibly strong she was. He took his foot and pushed against the washing machine, propelling them both backwards until she slammed into the wall and he broke free.

"This ends NOW, Michelle! It's over! You need to leave!" He yelled loudly, hoping she wouldn't notice the shakiness in his voice.

The slap she delivered was sharp and unexpected, but it was surely her way of egging him on and riling him up even more. Blow after blow, she pummeled his chest with her fists - surprisingly, each punch had enough weight behind it to cause a bruise, and he didn't expect that coming from a woman. He mentally corrected himself, besides the fact that this wasn't the time to be misogynist, she surely wasn't a woman either.

She paused her attack and stared him down, daring him to hit back, and he almost didn't. Until he remembered all he had to lose if he didn't finish this today.

"What are you waiting on, BITCH?" She curled her lip and snarled at him.

When he threw the first punch at her face and connected with her nose, it was almost as if he were standing outside of his body and watching someone else do this horrible thing. He heard the crack of bone but he pulled back his fist and punched the same broken nose again and again until the blood covered her chest. She looked at him with something like shock in her eyes, and perhaps a hint of fear, he thought to himself, but he couldn't let her throw him off guard with the acting. He had a job to do.

He threw a solid punch into her midsection, bending her over with her hands covering her belly; that gave him the chance to uppercut and send her flying backward over the threshold and into the living room. When she landed on the coffee table, dazed, she looked up at him through blood-filled eyes and opened her mouth to that gaping black hole that frightened him days before.

"Is that all you got, Bozo? You can't killll-llll me, Willlllll," she continued to scream, even as her head hung over the side of the coffee table at an unusually awkward angle. "You can keep trying but you can't killll me!"

Will stood glaring at her crumpled before him, his chest heaved and his lungs hurt. He caught his reflection in the mirror on the far side of the room and he barely recognized the man looking back at him. He had just finished beating a woman within what surely had to be the end of her life, yet she wailed at him and taunted him as if he'd just tickled her.

"You can't killll me, baby!" She said, her eyeball flopped against the side of her cheek; she raised a bloodied hand and carefully pushed it back into the socket. "Ain't you figured it out yet?"

"Figured what out?" He panted, tired and frustrated – and scared.

She laughed heartily. "I'm already dead, bitch!"

She howled and pulled herself to her feet again.

Will knew one way he could slow her down, even if it was only temporary. The key was to make sure she couldn't get back up this time. If she was out long enough that he could drag her to the shed, it would be her last time coming back.

———ele———

"So, this is her, right there?" Dodge pointed at the case at Will's feet.

Will nodded. "Part of her. I don't know which part. I had three cases. I left the other two down the road, in different places. One in the woods, the other in concrete. This one –"

He kicked it, it kicked back.

"I don't know what's in here, not enough to sit out on the porch and greet the neighbors. But apparently enough to keep raising hell."

The case shook violently, almost tipping itself over. Will kicked it again.

Dodge felt something like fear inside of his veins. And not a lot of things scared him, but this was something he never would have believed if he didn't see it with his own eyes.

"What do you think she is, or was? Or...is?"

"I have no idea. If I had to guess, wherever she went when she died a long time ago, she never came back. This-"

Will touched the case gently.

"I don't know what this is. It's not my wife's sister, I know that much."

Will slid off the stool and pulled the case to his side. He pulled a wad of bills from his pocket and tossed them all on the counter. "This is for both of us. I appreciate you listening to me tonight. I guess I needed someone to bear witness to this madness, and you seem like a guy who understands madness so I'm glad it was you."

Dodge watched as Will pulled a long chain from a deep pocket inside of his coat. The men exchanged knowing glances as Will secured one end of the chain to the handle and wrapped the other end around his fist.

They shook hands and Will even waved goodbye to the server before heading to the door, dragging his case alongside him.

Dodge chugged the bottom two fingers of his glass and slammed the empty glass on the counter. He covered it with his hand when the bartender headed in his direction.

"I'm good, my man," He stood up and stretched, realizing for the first time how long he'd been sitting on the stool. "Hey, nice place you've got here, by the way."

"Thanks, I'll let Daddy know," the bartender replied with a head nod.

By the time Dodge made it to the parking lot, he could barely make out Will's dark outline, walking slowly away from the bar, ambling down the dirt path which, according the sign, lead toward the bay. By the soft light of the lamp post, Will appeared to be a very old man, bent over and dragging the rolling luggage behind him. Even from the distance, Dodge could see the heavy chain looped around Will's waist, on the outside of his coat, and connected to the case.

Dodge sighed and reached into his pocket to caress the handle of the steel revolver. He'd dropped a lot of bodies in his time, yes, but tonight he had a chill in his bones and it wasn't from the cold. He got into his car and drove slowly across the lot to the embankment and parked with his low lights aimed in that direction. If nothing else, he could sit and watch and be ready with his finger on the trigger.

In case the bitch still wouldn't go.

Men Don't Leave

THEY SAY THAT NEW love is the best love, but the love that Travis Whitley felt for his wife still burned hot after thirteen years.

He'd met Sunny during Parent-Teacher conferences when she swept into his classroom like a tornado, an hour late for their meeting; with her wild curly hair piled into a messy bun, limping on a broken shoe heel, and filling his classroom with the scent of cocoa butter – he fell so deeply in love that it made his heart ache. Literally. He stood up to greet her, then clutched his chest and fell to the floor, striking his head on the edge of his desk on the way down. Hours later, he came to in a hospital bed and the first thing he saw when he opened his eyes was the face of an angel.

Then he heard Sunny's voice speaking from the corner of the room, behind the beautiful nurse hovering over his bed to check his vitals.

"It's about time you woke up – I've had a hell of a day and you having a heart attack didn't help." Sunny scoffed as she stood with one hand on her hip.

Travis knew then that Sunny was the woman he was going to marry.

The fact that her son was one of his most challenging students only helped cement his love for her and his sympathy for her struggle as a single mother. Like most first graders, six-year-old Jaxx was only interested in lunch and recess, and then tried to float through the rest of the school day. But he really came alive when it was time to run and toss a ball on the school playground, so Travis introduced the idea of getting Jaxx involved in Pee Wee Football to teach him social skills with the benefit of burning off some of his nervous energy.

It worked. And Sunny was grateful for the advice and assistance provided by Travis; so grateful, in fact, that eventually the awkward silence at the end of their consultative phone calls gave way to an invitation to dinner.

The rest – as the saying goes – was history.

Jaxx's father had checked out of their lives around Jaxx's fifth birthday. He just left, walking out the back door without so much as a *'Later, gator'*. Less than a year later, Travis stepped in and became the husband that Sunny needed and the father that Jaxx didn't know he needed. While it wasn't easy taking over a ready-made family, it gave Travis PURPOSE. Purpose and a sense of belonging that he hadn't felt in many years. He understood their situation better than most, because his own father had abandoned their family when he was very young and he witnessed his mother working herself into an early grave to support them. At 15, he stood at her gravesite and vowed that if he were ever blessed with a family of his own, he would never intentionally leave them under any circumstances within his power.

They discovered a few years into the marriage that Sunny was unable to have any more children, but that was okay because they had Jaxx. Travis felt blessed to watch Jaxx grow from a scrawny, quiet child into a star football player and hulking athlete who towered over both Travis and Sunny. Together, they formed a family that was admired and envied by all who encountered or had the pleasure of knowing them.

Travis pulled his car alongside the drive-thru speaker and pressed the button to lower his driver side window.

"Welcome to Burger Shack. May I take your order?"

"Um, just a minute, please," he replied, squinting his eyes to read the menu. He needed glasses badly. And perhaps surgery to repair his torn retina. But until then, he squinted.

"Do you have any breaded chicken sandwiches? I see grilled but not breaded..."

An audible sigh came through the speaker. "If you don't see it then we don't have it, sir."

Travis looked across the street at a competitor's fast-food restaurant and considered driving there instead, but he could clearly see that their drive-thru lane was already wrapping around the store and it would take much longer to get home.

"Are you ready to order, sir?" That annoyed voice again; clearly, she had better things to do. The car behind him bumped its horn and Travis felt his anxiety level rising.

"Okay, okay, sorry – just give me the chicken sandwich combo, please," Not feeling too confident with his selection, he reasoned that the time consideration made it the best choice.

"That will be $7.25, sir," the cashier announced as she pushed open the double window and gave him a dry stare.

Holding a ten-dollar bill in one hand, Travis fumbled through the change in his console until his fingers closed on a quarter. When he turned back to pass it through the window, the cashier's eyes were fixed on the deep angry scar on the side of his throat. He shifted in his seat and used his left hand to tug at his collar and cover the scar. She looked into his face with concern, then smiled softly, knowingly, and turned to complete his order. Her demeanor changed in that wordless moment, and when she returned to hand him the bag of food and drink through the window, her fingers touched his, briefly and deliberately.

"Have a good day, sir," she said and smiled again.

Travis found Sunny in her usual spot on the living room sofa, watching another one of her reality shows and arguing with the characters on the screen. She barely turned her head to acknowledge his return, but she did stick out her hand to accept the bag of food. "Took you long enough, I'm starving to death!"

Gingerly placing her drink on the cocktail table, he leaned over to plant a kiss on her forehead as she stuffed fries into her mouth and dug into the bag for the chicken sandwich.

"What's this?" She exclaimed, peeling back the paper and scowling at the beige meat peeking out from the bun. She picked off a corner of the chicken patty and touched it with her tongue before dropping it back in the bag.

"Grilled? GRILLED chicken? Why the fuck would I want GRILLED chicken when I'm eating french fries? Do you think I'm on a diet or something? Are you saying I SHOULD be on a diet?" Shredded lettuce flew from the wrapper as she angrily shook the sandwich at Travis.

"No, of course you don't need to be on a diet, sweetie, but that's the only type of chicken they had," Travis explained.

"Then why didn't you go somewhere else?"

"It would have taken longer! I knew you were waiting and didn't want you to have to wait longer."

"So, you got me SHIT instead? Something I don't want?" Sunny stomped over to the garbage can, dropping the sandwich inside.

"Look baby, I can fry you some chicken if you just let me get my stuff put away and do my lesson plan for tomorrow – then I promise I will fry you up some chicken, okay?" pleaded Travis.

Sunny waved her hand in his direction. "Don't worry about it. I'll just eat these fries and go get my own damn food. Gee whiz."

"I'm really sorry, hon. You should have told me earlier and I would have taken a different way home then I could have hit the Chicken Castle, they always have every kind of chicken you want."

"Whatever," Sunny resumed attacking the fries and watching the women on the television screen yell and throw drinks at each other. "Get that bitch, Tammy!" She screeched, ignoring Travis as he stood behind her.

Ashamed at his failure, he backed out of the living room and headed down the hallway to freshen up before beginning his evening routine of grading papers and preparing the lesson plan before dinner.

The first blow sent him crashing into the wall; blood spurted from his nose as his face slammed into the surface and he slid downward into a heap on the floor. Sobbing, he cupped his face to stop the flow spilling down the front of his shirt.

"No, wait, let me– "

He braced himself as he caught the whir of a boot-clad foot flying toward his face. He moved his hands to protect his eyes as the boot made contact with the side of his head. Pain shot through his temple and his vision blurred from both the pain and the blood smeared from his hands.

"You stupid fuck! Can't you do anything right?"

"I'm sorry," sobbed Travis, straining to look up at his attacker.

Jaxx straddled him with balled fists, yelling and spitting as he berated the broken man.

"What's so hard about getting an order right? Are you stupid or just dumb?" Jaxx yelled, delivering another round of blows about Travis's upper body.

"I'll go back and get it right this time! I'm sorry, please don't hit me again!" Travis cried, curling himself into a fetal position to protect his body from the assault.

Jaxx paused and took a step back, breathing heavily as if he'd just finished his daily five-mile jog.

Travis was afraid to even peek at him through his fingers so he remained still and prayed that it was over, that this beating would be quick and the pain fleeting. He heard a *click*, and then felt a slight breeze as Jaxx swung his arm and buried the blade in his stomach, twisting for good measure. Travis lay still and prayed soundlessly for mercy; he thought for a moment that mercy had arrived in the sound of Jaxx's boot stepping backward, but as usual, mercy skipped over him and Jaxx jumped forward to deliver a final kick to his stomach.

"Get it right next time – don't make me do this to you again, man," Jaxx spit at him, before turning and retreating from the room.

Jaxx was 10 years old the first time he killed his stepfather.

It began with an argument about the overflowing trashcan in the kitchen. Jaxx – who had grown nearly a foot since Travis moved in – stood defiantly with his arms crossed, refusing to budge in his resistance at taking the garbage to the cans in the backyard.

"You have so few chores around here, Jaxx. I think I've been more than fair," Travis said with a heavy sigh.

"Why don't you just do it and say I did?" Jaxx snarled at him and dropped his arms to his side, taking on a defensive stance. His eyes were dark and angry, much too angry for a ten-year-old, thought Travis, and the look on Jaxx's face disturbed him deep inside.

But he shook his head, dismissing the troubled feeling in the pit of his stomach; he turned around and began unloading the dish-washer.

The boy screamed as he closed the space between him and leaped on Travis' back, reaching around to pummel the man's face with his small, bony fists. Travis yelled out for Sunny, mostly out of shock at the attack, but there was a twinge of fear in his voice as Jaxx took him down the floor. He struck the open door of the dishwasher and the cutlery tray tipped and spilled across his chest, scattering across the ceramic tiled floor.

Jaxx was squeezing his neck so tightly that he couldn't move, but his head was facing the doorway and he saw Sunny's slippered feet standing there. *Standing still.* Just two white furry slippers with foam rabbit ears perched atop each foot, standing there. His eyes clouded in disbelief and he felt Jaxx move one hand to grapple for something that fell from the dishwasher. Then he felt the plunge of the knife in the side of his throat.

———*ell*———

Travis waited at least half an hour before unwrapping his limbs. He knew better than to move too fast or Jaxx may return, sensing that his message had not been effectively delivered. Travis often wondered if the steroids Jaxx injected were sharpening his hearing along with his muscle mass, because Jaxx would somehow always just KNOW when Travis stood up after each assault, and sometimes he would return with strength anew. So, Travis learned to wait until he heard the boy slam his bedroom door and turn on his television, only then did Travis feel safe enough to attempt to rise from the floor and drag his brutalized body down the hall to the bathroom.

He started a hot shower while undressing, then surveyed himself in the full-length mirror behind the bathroom door. His battered frame was a roadmap of his life – and his deaths; each of the hideous gashes and roughly healed bruises served as a testament to his commitment to stay and be the man his father couldn't. Sometimes, when the light faded to dark in his head and he felt life draining from his body, Travis would find himself wondering how much more he could take; when Jaxx might finally land the one strike that would permanently turn off his lights. But then that light would flicker and he'd feel himself being pulled back into the world.

He wasn't entirely sure that a part of him didn't wish for that eternal darkness.

But he wouldn't leave. No one could ever say that he'd left.

Originally appeared as "Men Don't Tell", Freestyle Friday, 7/2017

Bruce Loves Mary

HE'D STUDIED HER SINCE he was a child; both the truth and the myth.

From unconfirmed accounts to verified carnage left in her wake; he'd tracked and followed her for nearly forty years of his miserable life. She was a mighty force, a fierce and unforgiving spirit who snatched the souls of those who dared awaken her. But to Bruce, she represented the deepest love one could feel, love so deep that you would let it steal the breath from your lungs in order to touch its lips to yours.

He craved that kind of love, twisted it may be, but something inside of his soul craved that kind of unbiased ask-no-questions kind of *love* that would consume him and end the suffering he'd been forced to endure each day on earth.

She was the one he'd selected to bring him peace, and Bloody Mary was the name by which she answered.

Earlier attempts to get her attention had failed. Perhaps there was too much light coming in through the bathroom window, or maybe she sensed he wasn't passionate enough in his pleas. She had to know what was in his heart, regardless of what tumbled from his lips. She wouldn't be fooled.

But this time would be different. He had meticulously prepared the room for her arrival, lining the tiny window with black trash bags sealed on the edges with electrical tape; once the door closed, the room would be pitch black, as dark as a tomb appropriately. She would come for him this time for sure, and he could finally experience the highest manifestation of pure love.

Bruce stripped naked and showered, then shuffled into the bedroom where he removed a plastic covered suit from his closet He tore into the bag with his fingers, ripping it from the hanger to expose the virgin wool-blend suit beneath. He'd emptied his life savings to purchase it, but the evening he had planned called for the most elegant of fabrics and he couldn't be bothered with budgets. Besides, after tonight, money would be a thing of the past.

The fabric felt comforting against his skin and a wave of excitement rushed through his body as he smoothed his hand down the front of the jacket. He wanted to look good for his queen's arrival.

Standing with one finger poised above the light switch in the tiny bathroom, he quickly surveyed the room one last time to be sure he was ready.

He was ready.

"Bloody Mary. Bloody Mary. Bloody Mary."

The room was quiet, except for the sound of Bruce's nervous breathing. He stared straight ahead and waited; sensing no movement, he tried again.

"Bloody Mary. Bloody Mary. Bloody Mary!" He whispered, more urgently this time.

Suddenly, a pin point of light began to radiate from the center of the mirror, growing in size as it swallowed the darkness and illuminated the bathroom. Sounds of moaning, gnashing and bloodcurdling wails emanated from the center and Bruce realized with a start that as he peered into the mirror toward the source of the screams, he may actually be looking directly into Hell. But he wasn't afraid because he sensed his precious Mary was stirring within.

Something moved deep in the center of the mirror as a figure cloaked in black advanced toward him. Thick black ropes of knotted hair draped around her heart-shaped face where red eyes penetrated skin the color of smoked almonds. A lizard-like tongue snaked in and out between her lips as she floated beyond the edge of the mirror and crossed into the room with Bruce.

"Yes! Yes! Please take me with you!" Bruce trembled and cried out to the woman levitating just above the sink. His bladder released as he stared directly into her fiery eyes and begged for death.

Wordlessly, she moved downward and the room became warmer with her presence. He strained upward, wanting desperately to be consumed.

A tear fell from the corner of his eye as he squeezed his eyelids shut and leaned back his head. For the first time in his miserable life, he would finally know love. He steeled his body and held his breath, waiting for her kiss, but instead he felt a slight warm breeze pulsing across his face and he realized that it was her breath on his skin.

He peeked out of one eye and found her face floating just inches away, their noses nearly touching. Her eyes were merely red orbs beneath razor-cut bangs and messy tendrils framing her face, but he knew she was staring at him, staring into him, into his soul. He returned her gaze and almost choked on a rush of emotion; he had the attention of his Queen.

Excitement traveled through his body and caused his legs to tremble. When her tongue snaked out between her chapped lips and she opened her mouth to yawn, Bruce thought he might collapse to the floor in shock.

"Well, say something, you oaf," His beloved Mary – *Bloody Mary* – was clearly agitated. Bruce was taken aback, not just by the fact that she was within his arm's reach and speaking to him, but that she had a voice at all. The Bloody Mary of folklore, of his own dreams, did not engage in pointless banter or even utter a single word. She swooped in and did her bidding with surgical skill and a complete lack of pathos. Yet, here she was, crouched on his sink and attempting to socialize with him. *Him.* A mere nobody.

It warmed his soul.

Her hand snaked out from beneath the dirty tattered sleeve of her gown and Bruce felt a punch to his chest. The power behind the strike was much stronger than her small hand appeared capable of, but he felt it just the same.

"You summoned me, now stop wasting my time!"

"But-but-I thought you were going to...*take me*..." Bruce stammered like an idiot.

"Take you? Take YOU?" She laughed; a yawning black hole opened beneath her nose. The tiny room filled with the stench of burning flesh and rich, wet soil. Even as Bruce stared into her gaping hole of death, he had to stifle the urge to dive in and swim deeper into the blackness.

She reached out again but this time she stroked his face. The skin of her hand was rough and scaly, the ragged edges scraped against the stubble along his jawline. Her head tilted sideways as she examined him with a scowl on her face, her thin lips quivered and the tip of her forked tongue danced along the slit. Her fingers dropped down to pat the lapel of his suit; then she cackled.

"You men are all so predictable. You want me to free you from your *pain*, right?"

"No, I'm not like the others. I-I-I *love* you!"

"*I love you!* Ha!" She mimicked him and he felt his heart sink. This wasn't the way he had imagined his meeting with the love of his life. He had played the scene over and over in his head for years and never had he even considered that she might *not* want him. After all, Bloody Mary was legendary in her exploits but never had he heard that she rejected any man that summoned her.

"I'm bored. All of you humans bore me. It's the same song and dance every time." She pushed herself off the sink and rose again in the air, floating just above Bruce's head and directly in front of the thin stream of light. He could no longer see her, but he could feel her presence cloaking him in the darkness.

As she bore down on him, he felt his passion quickly turn to fear and he had an uneasy feeling creeping through his chest, telling him that his plan had gone terribly wrong. She wasn't the lover he'd anticipated, the one that would take him without question and return his love with an eternal embrace. Instead, she taunted him and made him feel unworthy of even her presence.

"I just want to love you," Bruce whispered. This time it was his bowels that gave way and soaked the pants of his mighty fine wool-blend suit.

"I don't need your love. I need your fear," Bloody Mary replied, drawing back and sniffing the air for the scent of his distress. It pleased her.

Bruce inhaled sharply as the specter swept him into her arms, crushing his windpipe and severing his spine in her deadly embrace. She held him until the twitching stopped, then let his body fall to the floor.

Her work completed, the bathroom mirror beckoned for her return, but whatever might lie beyond the taped door felt much more intriguing. She floated up and retreated into the corner of the ceiling, drawing her gown around her into a cocoon.

When the tiny stream of light through the window turned to darkness, it would be safe to explore.

And so, she waited.

Originally appeared as "Bloody Mary", Freestyle Friday, 10/2017 ; also appeared in Sirens Call eZine, Issue 43, 2019

Unfuck Me

"Alone again, naturally."

Ironically, the "70s Rock of Love" playlist was Amarie's go-to when she was feeling the most disgusted and disillusioned with love. In those moments of heartache, she could be found swaying to the tunes of Journey or Fleetwood Mac. Odd only because she wasn't even alive in the 70s, but she had a playlist of the music that took her to the place in her head where she needed to be. That place where she could escape from the pain and disappointment of real life and lose herself in the lyrics and melodies.

Lying on her bed in the darkness, the opening strains of "Dreams" by Fleetwood Mac poured into her earbuds and she couldn't help but chuckle at the irony of the lyrics.

"Now here you go again, you say, you want your freedom, well, who am I to keep you down?"

It's like...it knows. It fucking *knows*.

A hopeless romantic, she was. Weren't we all? At some point? Until the other shoe falls? Then you pick that bitch back up and put it on again?

The soft glow from her phone cast an eerie light against her troubled face as she swiped through the screens. HE was weighing heavily on her mind, even though she swore she didn't care, but she did; it didn't hurt, but it did. *Damn him to hell – damn his whole family to hell!*

Hot tears blurring her vision, she scrolled through photo after photo reliving happier times with Markus. They looked so in love, so content. How did it go wrong? He wasn't her first boyfriend by far, but breaking up with him left her shaken, challenging her entire worldview, and questioning herself, her judgment, and men, as a whole. There had surely been several messy and painful breakups since college. All of them were assholes, but some in particular had been nothing short of cruel, cheating on her even after having long *transparent* conversations about loyalty and the high currency of trust. Others simply drifted away, slowly – what you might call *ghosting*, until the relationship died a quiet death. But Markus? That one cut the deepest. He seemed so passionately connected to her...until he wasn't.

Oh, he was so smooth, that one. She shook her head – at herself – as she wryly recalled how he would casually leave his phone lying around, unlocked; even asking her to keep it for him while he tended to business at times. That was supposed to be a sign that she could trust him, right? Surely a man so unguarded with his phone wouldn't be cheating, because...how? It never occurred to her that a man so unguarded with his phone might have a second phone tucked away, someplace close, still within *his* reach, but quite out of *her* reach.

That last night, he made a tear-filled confession that he'd done some soul-searching and realized he just wasn't the right man for her. Fine, she could accept that. They cried together and parted ways. A couple of weeks later, she reminded herself to go and delete him from her social media apps, and she was confronted with pics of him in an outdoor wedding. As the groom. Getting fucking *married*. TWO. WEEKS. LATER.

"Babe, I'm leaving, I must be on my wayThe time is drawing nearMy train is going, I see it in your eyesThe love beneath your tears."

LIAR. She wished nothing but death and destruction to him. And his wife, she didn't care. They could go to hell together.

Through blurry eyes, she clicked through her phone's storage and deleted each image of Markus. Whether he was alone or posed in a group of friends, or even hugged up and laughing with her, he had to go. Just looking at his face – especially his happy face – caused a rumbling rage to fill her chest.

Just as she moved her hand to the bottom of the screen to close the Photos album, she noticed a curious glowing heart-shaped icon that she'd never seen before. Weird, she said aloud while thinking that it must have installed as part of a recent update. Tapping the icon opened up a simple interface with bold letters spelling out 'Unfuck Me' and words scrolling across the screen, *Undo the knot that binds your heart. Erase him from your story.* Shocked at first, she began to howl with laughter as she realized that it had to be a joke app installed by her bestie Taylor.

The app was unassuming and dead simple to use; it presented input fields asking for the full name, birthdate, and length of the relationship. Its icon was a simple puffed heart crisscrossed with stitches and traced with a faint, ethereal glow, yet it beckoned her with a strange allure.

"Unfuck me? Oh my God, this is hilarious!"

Intrigued and desperate for solace, Amarie tapped the first field and began entering the basic details about Markus. At the bottom of the form, an unsettling disclaimer warned: 'By entering a name, you agree to permanent erasure without any possibility for reversal. Effects may transcend the intended target.'

"Ha, whatever, show me!" Amarie giggled and tapped Continue.

Another warning popped up: 'Use of this application confirm your acceptance of the terms.' The screen presented two checkboxes asking her to acknowledge that she had fully read the conditions and that she agreed. She took a moment to scroll up and down to see if there were any terms displayed but there didn't appear to be anything other than what she had already blown past. She hovered her thumb over the Submit button as an internal battle played out between curiosity, temptation and fear. Curiosity won out and she tapped Submit, stomach lurching simultaneously with anticipation and dread.

Audio whispered through her phone's speakers, "Undo the knot that binds your heart. Erase him from your story."

In an instant, the room spun and blurred, distorting all around her. Scenes and memories of Markus rewound like a cassette tape, each moment unraveling in reverse. The laughter, the arguments, the tearful goodbyes – all retraced their steps, leaving behind an emptiness that mirrored the void within her heart. Amarie gripped her head to steady the spinning, feeling queasy. She pulled herself off the bed and stumbled through the apartment searching for relief from the discomfort. Moments later, she swallowed some Tylenol and collapsed on the sofa gripping a bottle of water in her hand. Perhaps just closing her eyes would make the uneasiness go away.

Amarie blinked rapidly and awakened to sunlight streaming through her living room window. Briefly, she had the flicker of a memory about doing something impulsive and funny the night before. What was it? Hopefully, not a drunk text! A twinge of horror and embarrassment rose to her cheeks as she tried to think hard to remember. Fuzzy remnants of the night danced at the edge of her consciousness but refused to take shape into anything solid. Whatever it was, it was gone now. Like when you have a kick-ass dream and you can't wait to wake up and tell somebody, then it evaporates as you awake.

She had no idea why she slept on the sofa. She didn't recall drinking any alcohol but her mind was certainly fuzzy. Shrugging it off, Amarie went to start her morning routine. Over coffee she scrolled through her social feeds. Selfies and brunch pics from her friends. Vacation snapshots from her parents' cruise. Nothing out of the ordinary - until she spotted Taylor, one of her best college friends, tagged at a restaurant with some guy she didn't recognize. *That bitch!* How could Taylor not tell her about this new guy in her life?

She switched the screen to call Taylor for the scoop on this mystery dude when she noticed something odd. Her call history over the past few months contained call after call with Markus Bell. At least one or two daily spanning months. But that name triggered nothing. No memories of conversations, inside jokes, or sensory associations came flooding to mind as they normally would for someone she apparently spoke with so frequently up until a few days earlier.

Tapping the number to redial, she listened to the shrill ring two times until it was abruptly auto-answered by a chipper recording: 'The number you have reached is not in service.'

Amarie felt uneasy now, grasping at the fraying edges of lost memories she couldn't retrieve. Was she too young for dementia? She'd read of some earlier cases, onset dementia it was called. The memory loss was extremely bothersome. She considered setting an appointment with her GP as she tapped on Taylor's name to auto dial her friend.

"Hey!" Taylor's familiar voice was instantly comforting. "What's going on girl? Why are you calling and not texting?"

"Oh, sorry, I hate when people do that to me too – weird kinda morning!" Amarie stammered. "Just saw your pics with that guy and realized we haven't talked in a minute. Hey, can I ask you something maybe kind weird?"

"You alright?" Taylor asked with an audible hint of concern.

Amarie took a deep breath before continuing. "Do you know someone named Markus Bell? Did I happen to mention him to you, ever?"

"Hmm..." Taylor paused, mentally scrolling back through their most recent conversations. "Not ringing any bells for me. Why? Who is he?"

Amarie felt her stomach lurch. Something very strange was at play here that she couldn't grasp.

"You still there?" Taylor asked.

"Uh, yeah, just trying to figure out why I have this number in my call history but I have no idea who it is. When I call, it's disconnected."

"Let's search his name, maybe he's a friend of a friend, hold on," Taylor quickly typed Markus Bell into each of her social media platforms. "Unless he's a white guy in Wales, or this old looking guy in Louisiana, I don't see anyone local by that name. Or anyone that looks like you might be chatting with him, unless you've got some freaky shit going on that I don't know about. Maybe it IS the old guy?"

"Very funny. Wait – let me see him," Amarie joked, laughing. "Just kidding. I guess I'll chalk it up to a fluke after the last update. It's always screwed up for days after those."

"Mine too. But yeah, about my date with Donovan. I was gonna text you today anyway. I like him! I mean, I like him a LOT! The question is, how he feels about me. Not sure yet. He ran a little hot and cold, mostly hot. I on like that...well, sometimes I do," mused Taylor. "Dating these days is straight hot garbage. Kinda tired of being in the game."

"I know, it's been a while for me too! The only dates I have these days are with the Doordash driver!"

"We have to change that soon. I'll see if Donovan has a friend and we can double-date!" Taylor offered.

"Sounds good, worth an effort, I guess. I'll talk to you later. I think I'm going to the gym," Amarie surprised herself but as the grogginess cleared, she realized that physically she actually felt pretty good.

"Whoa – the actual *gym*? Like, the place with the machines and stuff? Or did you mean Jim, like Jimmy's Grilled Subs? Because I will head over and go to Jimmy's!"

Amarie laughed heartily. "Nah, I mean I'm going to work out. Probably need to pay my membership again but I feel like I have a burst of pent-up energy all of a sudden. Let me go stretch and shower and get to the gym before I change my mind!"

At the gym, Amarie pumped her arms and walked briskly on the treadmill. She tuned the built in display screen to the local news, connected her earbuds, and allowed her mind to wander back to the mystery of Markus Bell.

Her entire call history suggested this Markus Bell had been a huge part of her life up until days ago. But suddenly all traces of his existence had been completely wiped from reality for her, Taylor, and who knew who else. He didn't even seem to exist online, therefore, he likely never existed anywhere. In her gut, a nagging that there was something disturbing related to the hazy half-recalled night before. But...*wait*...she was also feeling more energetic and alive than she had felt in...well, years!

She looked at the dashboard and was shocked to see that she was walking at a speed of 3.5mph – which may not seem like a lot but it was quite a boost for the couch surfer she had become over the last 3 years or so. Just being at the gym was a huge accomplishment, even if she did have to renew her membership at the desk because her key card no longer worked.

Feeling encouraged, she raised the incline – something she never attempted, but today, she just felt like she could do it.

And she did.

45 minutes later, she hit the Stop button and marveled at her results: three miles, 350 calories burned. Amazing, for a woman who would only pick up the mail once a week because she didn't feel like walking to the mailboxes.

As she leaned on the support bars to catch her breath, a news headline caught her attention and she tapped the volume button to turn up the sound.

Announcer: A   COMMUNITY MOURNS AS A LOCAL FAMILY IS FOUND SLAUGHTERED IN THEIR OWN HOME.

Newscaster: Channel 7's Hank Clifford is live on the scene – Hank, what can you tell us about this absolutely shocking tragedy!

Hank: Diana, I'm out here in Riverside, a quiet, upscale neighborhood that is struggling to understand just who would do such a thing. I'm speaking now with a neighbor to the victims -

Neighbor: "This kind of thing never happens here! I don't know what's going on but we're all scared to death right now!"

With a shudder, Amarie removed her earbuds and turned off the connection to the television.

"The world has gone mad," she sighed, bending into a deep squat to stretch her leg muscles.

Later in the evening, she thought about Taylor's offer to double date and she opened her phone to shoot her a message. Her eyes fell upon the same strange app that she'd opened the night before, right around the time she passed out from sheer exhaustion.

Her fingers hesitated over the icon, trembling slightly. Her memory was still fuzzy but something about the app ignited a fire inside of her and she felt compelled to tap it, or, tap it again.

UNFUCK ME
Undo the knot that binds your heart. Erase him from your story.

She chuckled at the audacity of the app making such wild and zany promises. While part of her thrilled at the thought of wielding such profound power. She clicked to continue and found herself confronted by the input fields.

"Oh, these guys are taking this seriously!" She laughed. "Let me think, who can I drop a curse on right quick?"

Amarie found herself drifting back in time, reliving the days before Clarke's toxic influence tainted her world and left her bitter and jaded. She hadn't even realized how much time had passed since she allowed herself to feel anything for anyone, that's how badly Clarke had burned across her soul.

Clarke Wilson stood six foot three and the first time she saw him she knew he would be her forever. He was charming, handsome, affectionate, and rich – so basically perfect, right? Except he also had a huge gambling habit, terrible with money (maybe due to the gambling habit or vice versa?) and was a pathological liar. That was a lot of bullshit wrapped up in that long lean body that she loved to curl up inside and forget about the world.

Until things started coming up missing around her house. Little things at first, little valuable things like her jewelry, her tablet, some gold coins inherited from her grandfather. Then she thought she was losing her mind when cash would randomly disappear from her purse.

Just thinking about it now, years later, still made her blood boil. He had played her for a fool, betraying her trust and her body through his own deception. She didn't give a shit that he had an addiction, that wasn't her burden to bear but he brought it to her and laid it in her lap and she hate him for it. His memory still ignited an emotional response and even though the little app was just a joke, she would give anything to be able to undo *that* knot and wipe him out of her life forever.

She typed Clarke's name into the field, along with his birthdate and the length of their past relationship. The next couple of screens contained the usual warnings and confirmations, probably similar to the privacy agreements in most other apps. Amarie clicked the boxes and blew past those, wanting to get to the end and see what kind of silly ad or subscription offer might appear. Instead, the screen began a swirling vortex of shapes and colors while eerie strains of a melody played through her phone's speaker.

Minutes later, a text message from an unknown number popped up along the top of her screen.

> For each soul you send away from your past, another soul returns to continue their future. Thank you for playing Unfuck Me.

A cold spike of fear pierced Amarie's stomach.

"What the entire fuck is this? A soul must return? Whose soul?"

Feeling the same lightheadedness that she experienced the previous evening, Amarie chose to remain on her bed this time, instead of wandering and ending up on the kitchen floor. Leaning into the fluffy pillows, she noticed the app had completing processing her silly request. The main screen now showed the boldly animated Unfuck Me damaged heart logo.

As the next few days unfolded in a surreal dance of past and present, as Amarie marveled at the subtle but obvious changes in her life.

She stirred awake, stretching and leaping from her bed with a vigor and spring that she hadn't felt in years. At the bathroom mirror, she gasped at her reflection, wiping her eyes and doing a double take.

"Bitch! You look good!" She exclaimed at her reflection.

The eyes staring back at her seemed brighter, more luminescent, and her entire face held a flawless glow and radiance like she hadn't seen since her teens. As she leaned closer to the mirror, tenderly touching her skin, she noticed her thick curly hair had a natural shine to it that she could normally only see after a color rinse and deep condition.

Buzzing with incredible energy, she felt a need to *move*, just *move*. The gym was definitely on the menu, but she felt like she might even add on a spin class today!

Yet, as she navigated through the routines of her day, a disquieting unease lingered in the air.

She was turning back time. Well, something was turning back time. Or, time was turning back – for her. With each day, she looked and felt years younger and the only thing that had changed was....

With an audible gasp, Amarie slowed her speed on the treadmill as hazy memories came to mind. Opening the app, having a little fun with it by entering names. *Whose name?* She couldn't remember. But the last few days had been the best of her adult life. Peace. So much peace. Good health. Restful sleep. Youthful glow.

And the only thing she could remember was playing with the app and falling into a deep sleep.

She finished her workout and rushed to her car. The Unfuck Me heart icon glowed eerily against the backdrop of her phone's color theme. Slowly, she hovered her finger over the heart and it began to pulsate as the app opened.

UNFUCK ME
Undo the knot that binds your heart. Erase him from your story.

This time, she noticed the word HELP at the bottom of the screen in tiny, bold print. Well, she certainly did need help! She tapped the link and a chatbot opened on the screen.

> *Welcome to Unfuck Me customer support. My name is Tom. How can I help you?*

> Hi Tom. I just have a couple of questions. I know this app is just for fun but I've been playing with it and I'm a little worried now.

> How can I help you?

> Does it really work? I mean, does it really erase people?

> Unfuck Me is for entertainment purposes only.

Amarie breathed a sigh of relief. "They had me really thinking they were erasing my boyfriends. It's a game, you idiot! It's just an app!"

She thought of another question for Tom and typed it into the field.

> But I can't remember any of the names that I put in.

> Unfuck Me is for entertainment purposes only.

She felt a knot in the pit of her stomach. If she couldn't remember who she erased, how would she bring them back?

> What if I want to reverse everything? Can I undo it?

> All erasures are permanent and cannot be reversed.

> Is there anything else I can help you with?

> Wait. The app says that for each soul I send away, another soul returns to continue its future. Where are those souls returning from?

Seconds ticked by with no response from Tom.

> ??

> Hell.

> Is there anything else I can help you with?

Frightened, frozen, and unable to type a response, Amarie stared at the screen and suddenly felt a dread that Tom might be able to see her.

She tapped the X in the upper corner of the window to close the chat, then threw her phone face down on the bed. Her hands were shaking. This couldn't be real. It's a fucking *app*.

It couldn't be real. Could it?

She pulled the edge of the blanket over the phone to hide it from her sight. But her hands wouldn't stop shaking.

elle

The next morning, Amarie tried to pretend that everything was fine; chopping vegetables for an omelet while keeping one ear tuned to the television on the kitchen counter. The local news anchor's voice drifted in and out until a certain phrase caught her attention.

"...horrifying massacre in the Lincoln Park neighborhood last night. The homeowners, Gregorio and Londa Wilson, were found in the basement with fatal injuries too violent to be described on our program."

Amarie set down her knife, feeling the hair rising on her arms despite the warm kitchen. Lincoln Park. That was only a few blocks away from her home.

The anchor continued with the shocking details but Amarie was in a daze; the icon of the Unfuck Me app spun in her mind, beckoning to her.

A rush of sudden realizations made her knees feel weak and she grabbed the edge of the counter to steady herself. Then she froze. A memory resurfaced, one that made her blood turn to ice. The timing lined up. She was playing with that mysterious app, just having fun, and then...someone dies. The words of Tom, the customer service bot, flashed before her eyes – *from Hell*. They were returning from Hell. And it was all because of her.

Amarie's pulse pounded in her ears and she wanted to cry. It had to be just an awful coincidence. And yet...she flashed back to other times recently when random chaos had occurred right after she'd used the app.

The implications were terrifying. How much unintentional harm had she caused in her selfish need for revenge?

Amarie realized she was trembling, clutching the counter for support. But how could she control something she didn't understand or even remember?

As the consequences of using the Unfuck Me app roiled around her, Amarie grappled with the realization that rewriting the past came at a cost far dearer than she could have ever imagined. She had returned to the app over and over, freeing herself of every regretful lover and erasing the trauma of their connection from her life. In doing so, she had restored her own youth and health, adding years to her life by removing most of the events that caused her stress and pain.

At the same time, the world around her was trapped in a frightening vortex of violence that may not have touched her, but she was the cause. Each day, the news reported seemingly random acts of violence that were unexplainable, with no logical connection or trail of the murderer – or, murderers.

Amarie's ghosts were erased, while the walking dead returned to wreak havoc on people she didn't know. The sacrifices made in the name of love and liberation demanded more than she imagined. But deep down, part of her was already contemplating entering just one more name, consequences be damned.

"I hate him so much!" Taylor cried, her chest heaving with anger and sadness. "How can someone just act like this? What is wrong with these men?"

Amarie was crushed. In the far recesses of her mind, she knew that she had once felt that same kind of heartache. The details were fuzzy, but she could feel around the edges of the memories.

Taylor choked back sobs as she confessed that while she realized Donovan was love bombing her, she fooled herself into believing he just might actually want something more than a sneaky link. Nevertheless, he'd stopped returning her calls and texts and eventually blocked her from his social media page.

"That dirty bastard," Amarie exclaimed. "It never ceases to amaze me how incredibly low some men will stoop."

"That's not all. I made a fake page so I could look at his page, I thought well maybe he took his social media down for work or something, right?"

"Okay, go on."

"Well, he was right there, hugged up with his girlfriend at the sunflower farm. And I scrolled back some months, I was apparently the side chick!"

Amarie's heart broke for Taylor. She wanted so badly to ease her friend's searing pain. She'd never experienced it herself but she knew that that kind of betrayal cut to your very core and left indelible marks.

Almost reflexively, Amarie reached for her phone and woke the screen, searching for the eerie app icon that had faded from her mind in recent rejuvenating weeks. Before she could stop herself, she wordlessly slid the phone in front of Taylor, the Unfuck Me app open and ready for another victim.

Taylor looked at her quizzically through eyes red from crying. Amarie pointed to the phone and nodded her head as realization washed over Taylor's face.

"What is this?" Taylor whispered, but Amarie silenced her with a determined stare.

"Just do it," Amarie whispered back.

The serious look on her face told Taylor that she was serious, and Taylor knew that her best friend wouldn't lead her in the wrong direction. She picked up the phone and looked closely at the screen. Slowly, she began to enter Donovan's information into the fields, she paused before hitting Submit. Amarie nodded again, urging her to continue.

Taylor tapped the Submit button.

The countdown began, that familiar chilling sequence reaching zero in seconds.

Across town, a chorus of bloodcurdling screams rose in the air.

The Iceman Cometh

"I HEARD YOU CREEPING around my door last night, you stupid cow," Bonni pushed me face first into the wall, twisting my arm behind my back as she whispered in my ear. "Don't do it again."

"What are you talking about? I didn't come near your door!" I managed to protest through my squashed lips, tasting the flat chalky latex paint on my tongue.

She pushed harder and pain shot through my lower arm into my shoulder. A single thought raced through my mind, she broke it, ohmigod, she broke it, and she slammed her knee into the back of my thigh in response.

"I heard you, the floor creaks outside my door, I know it was you, you fat shit!" Her tongue snaked out and licked across my ear-lobe before she released me. I crumpled to the floor, holding my throbbing arm across my chest.

Bonni stepped back and delivered a fierce kick to my ankle with her gym shoe-clad foot, then she twirled around and danced down the hallway away from me. I watched her back as she wiggled away, stretching her arms out to touch the walls and humming to herself. I waited until she disappeared into her room and slammed the door, then I examined my arm, propping it across my knee.

It wasn't broken, I surmised, as there were no bones poking out, but the visible swelling told me that it was indeed sprained. Fat chance on getting to a doctor. Mama didn't do doctors unless there was an imminent death and if you even asked, you might get a busted lip out of the request. I pushed myself up from the floor with my one good arm and went to my room to retrieve a box from the bottom of my closet.

The old shoebox had the words Repair Kit written across the lid in crayon. I had deco-rated the shoebox lid when I was 7. I was almost 15 now but I still kept my tools inside, the tools I needed to fix the pieces of myself that Bonni continued to break. Inside, there was plenty of gauze, band aids, antibiotic spray and iodine to clean and cover the many cuts and bruises she inflicted when she was feeling playful. There was also a cloth bandage that I'd shoplifted when Bonni pushed me down the stairs and I sprained my ankle. I'd even learned how to crudely stitch the stab wound in my leg, from the time she thought I'd mouthed off to her. I had in fact not mouthed off to her but facts didn't matter when it came to Bonni.

Too bad there was nothing in the box that could fix my heart.

It was a way of life, living in the same house but staying out of her way. I wistfully counted down to the year she would finally leave, off to college or wherever she decided to go after finishing school, but I anticipated peace in my home for the first time since...well, since I was born.

They say babies don't have memories but I swear I remember her face leering over mine, and I remember feeling afraid, and I remember crying and no one came.

That was life with Bonni. But for some reason, I loved her evil ass.

I woke up for my nightly bathroom break and heard those same muffled sounds coming from Bonni's room on the other side of my bedroom wall. Disturbing sounds like panting and moaning and guttural noises that made me unsure if I should try to help her, or jump out of bed and run away. I'd heard those same noises the night before and I tried to investigate but chickened out before I got to the source.

After having my arm bent back earlier in the day, I was afraid to even get out of bed to go to the bathroom, so I just sat up, listening closely. Had she fallen asleep with the television on again? Was she keeping an animal in her room - did she secretly have a pet when Mama wouldn't allow *me* to have a pet?

The noises grew louder and more intense, so I quietly slipped out of bed and tiptoed across the length of space between our rooms. As I got closer to her door, my stomach began to turn in fear of what I might see and what I might suffer at her hands if she caught me.

My hand trembled reaching for the doorknob. I knew I was risking everything but I had to find out! Just a peek and then I'd scoot on down to the bathroom and back to minding my own business.

Holding my breath, I turned the knob slowly, carefully. The door inched open smoothly, without so much as a squeak. I pressed my eye to the opening and waited for my sight to adjust to the figures moving around in the darkness.

My mouth went dry and I clamped my lips together to hold back a gasp. I couldn't tell for sure where Bonni was in the room, but there were moving figures on the bed illuminated by the bluish glow of her aquarium light. A strange, hulking form that threw an even larger shadow against the wall as it bent forward and mounted the figure beneath it. It balanced itself with huge arms rippled in muscles – one which looked to be larger than my entire body. As its head turned wildly from side to side, I spotted horns pointing toward the ceiling, and slitted eyes resembling shiny steel, glinting in the dim light. It threw back its huge head and moaned and howled, and I was both repulsed and fascinated.

Now, I wasn't a child, I was certainly old enough to comprehend what I was witnessing, but the depravity of *this* was beyond my understanding. I wanted to scream Bonni's name to get her attention but even though I couldn't see her, the sounds coming from the figure on the bed told me that she wasn't in need of my help.

At least, she didn't think she was.

The horned (and horny) demon at the back of her kind of made me think she needed my help.

As I stared through the opening in the door, contemplating my next move, the creature collapsed onto the bed and positioned its large head onto Bonni's lap as she sat against the headboard.

By the soft light, I could see that she was gently stroking its matted fur and I could hear it *purring*, loud and rumbly like a rock inside of a soda can. I cringed at the thought of its purring waking Mama and then I'd be in trouble for peeping into Bonni's room. It didn't go unnoticed that she now handled this beast with far more love and tenderness than she ever showed to me.

I pulled the door closed, slowly, softly; the rattle of the purring disguised the click of the doorknob and I was able to escape back to my room. firmly behind me as I hurried back down the hall. My mind reeled as I crawled back into bed. I could still hear the purring through the wall near my head, and after a while, it lulled me to sleep.

———*ele*———

Looking back, I think I always knew that my sister was evil. It was nothing that I could prove. I certainly couldn't go to our mother with my suspicions because she was far and wide my mother's favorite. Any time I tried to lodge a complaint, I would be shut down with that look that said, *I ain't got time for your pain.* If I insisted on pursuing the matter, a sharp slap across the bridge of my nose taught me to keep my tears to myself.

Bonni would sit across from me at the dinner table and leer at me above the top of the floral centerpiece. Her lips stretched into a nasty grimace that enjoyed my discomfort and made me promises of pain. Mama missed it all. She kept her eyes fixed on her plate, angrily shoving forkfuls of meatloaf into her face and scraping the fork with her teeth as she withdrew. Mama missed everything except the things that I did to Bonni, she always caught those. Because yes, sometimes, I did things to Bonni too.

I would get tired of her, just downright tired, and I would do sneaky things like steal her makeup and put it in the garbage. Once, I even cut her hair while she was sleeping, then played innocent about it. That was worth the beating she gave me because I was only sore for a day but it took months for her hair to grow back. Ha!

I never figured out *why* she was so fully committed to being nasty and vile and un-compassionate. What part of her brain clicked on - or off - and decided that she should operate under this veil of dark energy? It never made sense to me because it had to take so much more effort to frown and scowl. And it confused me because all I ever wanted was for her to *see* me, but my presence was always met with contempt.

But after what I'd learned last night, I now had a chance to either win her over by saving her, or make her hate me even more by snitching.

I mulled it over and decided to snitch. After all, I couldn't be expected to fight that monster alone.

I waited until Bonni had left the house to go do...whatever it was that she did when she left the house, probably squeeze the nostrils shut of newborns at the hospital. Wouldn't be surprised at all.

I found Mama at the dining room table and I launched right into my story.

"Bonni had someone in her room last night!" I said, breathless with excitement. "I heard her and then I saw her!"

My feet were moving back and forth, almost dancing with anticipation of her angrily unleashing a tirade on Bonni and finally punishing her to the high heavens.

She snapped her head toward me, fire in her eyes as she stared at me. (yes! yes!)

"What the hell are you talking about?" She asked. Her face was framed by brown pin curls sticking out from beneath her satin bonnet. In the soft light coming through the kitchen window, she had an almost angelic glow to her skin. But I knew better, and I decided to choose my words carefully.

"I heard something last night. Really, I've been hearing things every night and I finally got up to look. And I saw her, Mama. She was doing...nasty stuff!" I opened my eyes as wide as I could and tried to look sincere and concerned.

"What do you know about nasty stuff?"

"Well, I'm not a baby. I know what I saw. And I'm pretty sure she wasn't supposed to have no man in her room, that's all I'm saying." I shrugged and turned my back on her, pretending to look through the cabinets for a bowl.

"I bet you were just confused. She knows better than to sneak someone in here. I don't believe it." Mama was shaking her head side to side.

I continued stalling by fixing a sandwich that I didn't even want, but I was hoping that Mama would ask more questions, get angry, *something*. But she eventually slid back her chair and left me in the kitchen alone.

I nibbled around the edges of the bread and tossed the rest into the garbage. Disappointment had soured my tongue and I knew that Mama was surely going to tell her what I'd said. Feeling defeated, I just wanted to go to my room and wait for Bonni to get home and deliver my beating.

Around midnight, the sickening sounds began rolling down the hallway to my sleeping ears. I rolled on my stomach and pulled my pillow over my head but I couldn't block out the howling, moaning and *slurping* noises. This time, it was even more obscene than before, louder, more aggressive, more...*moist*.

I shivered and sat up in bed, still holding the pillow around my head.

I didn't want to see.

But I had to see.

Something was different this time. Were they taunting me? I didn't know but I had to see.

Bonni's bedroom door was already cracked open when I approached. The colorful melting wax of the lava lamp illuminated the darkness, and my eyes followed my ears to the noises, eventually focusing on the moving figures on the bed.

It didn't take long to identify the source of the shrieks and wails. I recognized the same horned beast from the previous night, straddling a woman bent over the side of Bonni's bed. But when the woman raised her head and turned her face toward me, I choked back a scream as my own Mother leered at me through the darkness.

Her face stretched into a grotesque mask of pain and pleasure, and she bared her teeth as if she were daring me to interrupt. My blood ran cold in my veins. My feet wouldn't move even though in my mind I was trying to get away. I heard a cough from the opposite corner of the room and I turned my head to see Bonni sitting in the chair, watching.

My stomach roiled. I forced my feet to move; stumbling down the hall and falling to my knees in front of the toilet. I heaved until my head hurt and crawled back down the hall to my bedroom.

—ele—

"Oh, Beale would love her little tight ass," Mama said, her voice dripping with malicious delight. She and Bonni sat on the sofa together, sizing me up from across the room as I stood at the sink doing dishes. I felt so violated as they jeered at me with obvious anticipation about presenting Beale with such a virginal gift. My skin crawled and I felt nauseous at their glee.

"You're right. He would be so pleased if we presented him with her as a gift!" Bonni's eyes were glazed over

Bonni's eyes were glazed over, her mind lost in thoughts of how much favor she would gain from my sacrifice. I could feel their eyes burning into my skin, their gazes raking over my body with lecherous hunger.

I felt like a piece of meat being inspected and prepared for consumption. My stomach churned with nausea as I realized that these women, who I once thought were my family, saw me as nothing more than a tool for them to get closer to their favorite demon.

Bonni raised her nose in the air and inhaled deeply and dramatically. "Mmmm, smell that, FRESH MEAT!" She giggled insanely.

My jaw clenched and my hands gripping the sink so tightly that my knuckles turned white. They were getting a sick thrill out of inflicting embarrassment on me and I wasn't going to let them enjoy that pleasure.

I finished cleaning the kitchen while they continued to sit on the sofa making jokes while giggling and falling over each other. After locking myself in my room, I waited until I heard them leave the house together before I snuck into Bonni's room to investigate.

How was this thing getting into her room? Was he coming in the front door? Did he drive there? Climb up the wall and enter the window? If I was going to find out, I had to do it quickly before they returned.

All I knew about demons, I'd learned from watching movies, and the one thing that I remembered was that they didn't like salt. Not just any salt but rock salt. The kind that Mama threw outside on the sidewalks in the winter time to melt the ice. Apparently, that kind of salt dissolved demons like acid – at least it did in the movie I'd seen. Would it work? I wasn't sure, but it was worth a shot. I couldn't go into her room empty-handed so I headed out to the garage and grabbed the 20-pound bag of rock salt leaning against the wall. Winter was a long way off, Mama had time to get more, I had demons to dissolve.

———*ele*———

It wasn't often that I got to enter Bonni's room. Usually, she would push or pull me in there to either question or pummel me in private. I stepped inside quietly, almost holding my breath; it felt like a privilege to be on the other side of the door but it also felt very dangerous. I began looking under the bed, behind the dresser, lifting up pictures to look behind them; I was searching for any strange points of entry, anything that looked out of place.

Or, anything that looked like it might be a portal to Hell.

I found it in her closet. She had it cleverly hidden, I almost missed it, but something about the way her clothes were sloppily tossed on the floor made me curious. Bonni kept a tidy room with everything in its place, yet there was a pile of laundry just dumped in the closet, it didn't seem right to me. I used my arm to slide over the pile of clothes and sure enough there lie a crudely cut square of wood slid over a gaping hole in the closet floor.

The walls on the inside of the hole were slimy and oozing with some type of thick milky substance. I could feel the heat radiating from deep within the hole but I was afraid to get too close to the edge for fear I'd fall in or be snatched in. But as I listened closely, I thought I heard faint screams and subsequent sobs from deep, deep within the hole.

Without further hesitation, I reached for the bag of salt and ripped open the bag, then pushed it toward the hole and let it tip over. The sharp gravel poured freely and steadily down into the hole. I used my foot to tap the bag and nudge it to continue whenever it slowed its spill.

The salt was almost gone when I heard a high-pitched whistle racing toward me; before I move, a large muscular arm of crimson skin came swinging up out of the hole, grasping around the edges in a desperate attempt to connect. The hand was as large as my head and the fingers were the size of a small child's arm. It flopped and clawed and gripped at the floor, leaving deep scratches in the wood as it drew back in anger.

I was scrambling backward on my hands and knees, trying to avoid being grabbed by that monstrous hand, when suddenly Bonni shrieked behind me in the doorway.

"NOOOOOO! WHAT HAVE YOU DONE?! She yelled, rushing forward and tossing herself at Beale's arm. He gripped her around her waist and howled a deep painful roar as he began to drag her toward the hole.

I panicked at the look of confusion and fear in Bonni's eyes. I think at, first, she wanted to go with her demon lover but as she started to tip into the hole, she realized that she would actually die if she went in.

I caught her leg with both hands before he could pull her waist over the edge; I pulled back with all of my strength – which wasn't much of a fight against a creature from Hell but he wasn't expecting any resistance.

The nearly empty bag of salt sat at the edge and I took my foot and kicked it, sending one last stream of salt down to land on the beast. He screeched and lunged upward once more. I could see his skin smoking and peeling from the contact of the salt on his skin.

I took advantage of the opportunity to reel back once more and gain more traction with Bonni. I wasn't going to let her go – not like this!

Suddenly, Mama raced into the room and ran past Bonni and I, screaming, "Take me instead!!!"

She dived directly into the hole, head first, taking the creature down with her. We could hear her screaming for a long time as she traveled down, down, down. Bonni curled into a ball and wept while I crawled over and pushed the cover securely back on top of the hole.

I collapsed on top it and finally let the tears flow.

I'd seen a lot over the past few months. Lost my mother to...well, a story that people wouldn't believe but she was gone. I'd saved my evil sister from a fate worse than death. I'd battled a demon from Hell.

But I've never delivered a baby.

Bonni was adamant that she didn't want to go to the hospital, so it was just me and my Repair Kit working overtime. After all, giving birth is one of the most natural things a woman can do. This should be easy peasy.

"Snap out of it, stupid ass! I think I need to push!" Bonni screamed, as she grabbed my hand and squeezed in a vice-like grip.

I jumped into action, loosening my hand from hers and positioning myself at the foot of the bed to guide her. My eyes were peeled for the little things, the baby's head crowning, the sight of horn stubble and crimson-tinged skin.

A mop bucket full of rock salt sat at my feet, just in case.

Just in case.

Lovesick

HE HELD ME TIGHT and said that he loved me, and it was wrapped in a velvety-throated whisper. That's what made me forget about the thing I said I wasn't going to do again.

I'd almost missed it when the words brushed by my earlobe, soft and wet like the tip of his tongue when he drags it across my nipple, during those times he's feeling playful and enjoys making me squirm. When I'm drifting away in a post-orgasmic haze, the way he often left me - spent, aching and begging for sleep. It had been a long time but I remembered too well.

He just wanted to be close to me for a little while, that's what he said. I scooted over and let him under the blanket, after all, he *was* my husband.

A long loop of his hair lay across my face while his heart beat a symphony in the palm of my hand squashed beneath his chest. Eyes closed, I inhaled the moment, savoring the smell of his skin and the sound of him breathing. I was full of love and hope and delusion, not quite thinking about tomorrow because I had become accustomed to the fact that tomorrow was going to do whatever it wanted to do. Today didn't matter; despite what they tell us in love songs, today really didn't shape tomorrow. My fate had already been sealed and this man right here was the orchestrator of my future.

I turned my head in his direction and a thick rope of his coarsely twisted hair fell away from my face and landed on my neck. Lately, I'd had a recurring dream about that rope snaking underneath my throat and wrapping tightly around my neck, pulling tighter and tighter until I woke up sweating and shaking. Holding it between my fingertips like a garter snake, I moved it away from my neck, then peered into the darkness for his face.

He moved quickly and climbed on top of me, whispering, "I love you. I love you. I love you."

"Donnell, wait. Get a condom."

He didn't wait and I didn't stop him. He knew how to make me forget what I was mad about, even if it was just temporary.

I didn't want to open my eyes because if I saw him looking at me, it would halt all of the delicious feelings and that lovely after-sex moment would end. We'd have to talk, and I didn't want to talk; I just wanted to lay there and smell him and feel him and mold my body into his. Knowing that once we exhaled, the disconnection would begin and I'd be alone again as soon as he peeled the covers away.

I felt him suddenly twitch, be still, then slide off, landing face down on the pillow.

"I just get so scared that you're gonna leave me," he said again.

"Why do you keep saying that?"

"Because I know you get tired and think about leaving."

Lightly kissing his arm, I tasted his sweat on my tongue and instead of salty, it was noticeably bitter.

"How about you stop making me tired? How about that?"

He didn't answer, instead he buried his face into my shoulder. I waited for him to slide out of bed and retreat downstairs to his hideaway.

I knew he was about to cheat before he cheated, because he told me.

He didn't really say those words but he told me with his *other* words. It was *me* who didn't listen closely enough. He came home complaining about a new girl in the restaurant. She was so stupid (according to him), she couldn't do anything right, he couldn't even understand how she got hired.

"They just hire anybody!" He'd ranted into the phone. "And then they always put them on my shift - why I gotta train the dummies?"

"I don't know, babe. Maybe they know you're going to train them correctly?" I tried to be supportive as I absentmindedly filed my nails.

"Well, I'm sick of this shit, they can make her somebody else's problem. I'm going to see if I can move her to another shift."

"Sounds like a plan," I agreed.

He continued to vent about this girl – Sophia was her name - she drove him crazy daily! He disliked her so much that he wanted her fired. Not only was she incompetent, but she was ill-mannered and had poor hygiene to boot, according to Donnell.

"Do you know what this fat bitch did today?" He started ranting as soon as he walked into our living room. "We're in the pantry going over the stock, just me and her, mind you, and she just let one rip, loud as day. Then started laughing! Can you believe that?"

He was disgusted and enraged. Hours later, as we got ready for bed, he was still shaking his head and telling me wild stories about her many failures at work and how he wished he could get rid of her.

And that's how I knew that Sophia was the one he was fucking this time.

After all, we'd been married for 15 years and I'd been through it often enough to recognize the signs. But I had been so focused on decorating our new home and trying to get myself in the healthiest condition ever so we could finally conceive before my last good eggs were gone. So, I missed all of the familiar signs of a new girl in his web.

After a few weeks had gone by, he'd layered on a good number of negative stories to convince me that Sophia was making his life miserable. Then he began working late to oversee kitchen clean-up and make sure the restaurant passed their inspections. Because he didn't want to disrupt my sleep by coming in late and showering off the "work smells", he began sleeping in the downstairs room on the occasional late nights. Those occasional nights turned into every night. The inspectors came and went, the restaurant passed, of course, because as much as Donnell worked, it had to be pretty goddamn clean.

And one night after his shower, he slid into bed behind me and wrapped me in his arms and kissed my neck and stroked my lips with his thumb (he knows I love that) and everything just felt safe again. The storm was over.

I asked no questions. I know. I'm a dumbass but I just wanted peace in my house again and I knew if I waited it out, he'd eventually get bored with Sophia like he got bored with all of the others.

"What's that, on your lip?" I pointed across the table with a frown.

We were enjoying the breakfast spread I rose early to make. The vibe was pleasant again, almost romantic; we laughed, we sang along with my R&B playlist, and he even helped me set the table. For the first time in a long time, it was a great morning in the Brinker household.

Until I spotted what looked like a huge flake of burnt sugar in the upper corner of his lip. I watched silently for a few minutes before calling his attention to it, because he kept passing his fork across it as he ate, yet it stuck in place. He drank from his glass and still that scab sat on his lip and it began to bother me because I could have sworn it wasn't there earlier. It wasn't there when he was laying with me and kissing all over my body – I would have felt it scraping me, right? My brain was screaming, *why don't you feel that? What's wrong with you?*

I jabbed my finger toward his face again, trying to hide my disgust – but it was pretty disgusting. My stomach started to churn.

"What *is* it?"

He looked confused for a moment, then his eyes followed the direction of my finger and he slowly reached up to touch his mouth. His eyes widened as he tenderly dabbed around the swollen, inflamed and angry-looking sore.

"Weird, I don't know what it is," Donnell replied with a shaky voice, before pushing back his chair and bolting from the table. He stumbled down the hall to the guest bathroom where I could hear the cabinet drawers being pulled open and slammed shut.

"There's stuff under the sink. Antibiotic ointment," I called behind him, trying to be helpful.

Donnell returned holding a bloody wad of tissue to his mouth. "I picked it off. It'll stop bleeding in a minute. I usually clot fast." He mumbled around the tissue trying to sound confident, but his eyes told me that he was terrified.

And just like that, my appetite was gone.

We met again for dinner at our favorite place – our own dining room. It was nice to be romantic again and look at each other over candlelight, in the quiet space of our home. After all, we'd built this house from the ground up and over the years the dysfunction of our marriage made it a less than desirable place to exist. But tonight, it felt like old times as we shared pizza and wine in the room we'd painted together.

Until Donnell – in the midst of retelling a joke - took a second or third bite of pizza, when suddenly his hands violently gripped the table and his body jerked forward as he projectile vomited across his plate, my plate, and the open pizza box. I froze, at first shocked, then amazed at the force, amount and speed of the expulsion; then finally, concern, as I jumped out of my seat in time to avoid being sprayed.

Donnell fell backward, shaking. I dropped to his side and placed my hands on each side of his face, I gasped at how deeply red the whites of his eyes had turned in those few minutes. Bloody inflamed vessels spread across each pupil and I immediately thought to myself, he's having a stroke or aneurysm of some sort.

On my knees, I scrambled back to the table and retrieved my phone which had just barely missed being destroyed by the contents of Donnell's stomach. I wiped the screen against my shirt and started to dial 911 when Donnell grabbed my hand tightly.

"Hold on, stop!" He whispered weakly.

"I'm gonna get you help!" I pulled my hand away and attempted again to dial.

"No! It's probably just a bug, like a 24-hour flu or something! You trying to get us a $700 doctor bill for the flu?" He pulled himself up from the floor, bloody eyes, putrid shirt and all. His legs were wobbly as he held on to the chair and tried to force a smile.

But even as he bared his teeth in an uncomfortable grin, his eyes said that he was terrified. Holding onto the walls, bumping the corners of photos and artwork along the way, he managed to drag himself through the house and into the guest room where he kicked the door shut behind him.

For the rest of the evening, I listened for Donnell to emerge from the room, but all I heard was muffled sobbing as if he were crying into a pillow. I should have checked on him. But I didn't. It sounds bad but I was so grossed out by the vomiting that I didn't even care that he was sleeping in another room.

※

I left him alone the next day as well. Part of me was concerned but the other part was also annoyed at the mess I had to clean up and how dare he be sick when he was already in the doghouse? Whatever he had, he could keep it with him in there.

Most of the morning, I stayed upstairs, keeping myself busy with chores and even napping.

Later, I could hear him bumping around in the room again. It was an awfully unsettling symphony, bringing to mind a wide-bodied animal loafing around the room knocking over furniture and dragging its soft furry body across the wood floor. I wanted to check on him; then again, I didn't care too much. I had one foot out of the door, tired of years of his disrespect and emotional abuse, rinse and repeat; at the same time, it wasn't easy to just

I tiptoed over to the door and pressed my ear against the wood, listening to the sounds of something dragging across the floor. The panel creaked a bit, just a bit, but the dragging noises stopped and a silence filled the other side of the door.

"Donnell? Are you in there?" I called out, and knocked lightly. "Why are you home?"

"I-I changed my shift. Going in later." He replied, softly. His voice sounded as if he were smothering, from deep within the blankets. Or his throat was full of mucus. I shrugged and went back to preparing my breakfast. It didn't appear that he had cooked anything or had even been in the kitchen, so I fixed him a plate and sat it on the table.

"I left you pancakes. I'm going back upstairs so you can pop out and grab them, okay?"

He groaned.

Once I got to the top of the stairs, he opened the door and sloshed across the kitchen tile with what sounded like wet feet. The plate scraped across the burner as he snatched it from the stovetop and slid back across the floor into the room, slamming the door behind him.

I tiptoed back down the stairs to peek into the kitchen, where the acrid smell of cigarette smoke hung in the air; I stopped abruptly on the bottom of the steps and crinkled my nose.

"Are you *smoking* in there, Donnell?" I yelled across the room toward the door, appalled at the thought.

Bump. Thump. Draaag.

"Donnell? Is that a cigarette?" I demanded this time. "Open this door."

Bump!

I tried to imagine the pieces of furniture in that room and what he could possibly be moving around – or bumping into.

Angry now, I jiggled the doorknob and of course found it locked.

"I'll get the key, Donnell! You can't keep me out!" In the kitchen and fished my hand around in the junk drawer for the plastic keyring. It wasn't there, and it was always there.

I went back to the door and kicked it with my foot.

"Open up now or I'm going to get the crowbar out the garage and pry it open!"

Just as I started to walk away, I heard the squeak of the door slowly opening; I spun around to see only part of his face peeking through the crack. One yellowed eye darted around before seemingly focusing on me as I stood at the door, confused and a little bit frightening. A clump of mucus caked the corner of his eye and a curtain of gunk hung onto the row of lashes. Finally, in a thick gurgling voice, he spoke.

"I smoke a little bit to take the pain away. The window is open. It won't bother you," he said and took a deep breath as if speaking drained his energy. His voice sounded as if he were talking through his teeth.

"Open the door, Donnell. I need to see you."

"No!"

A tear fell from that one infectious looking eye, he blinked and the gunk stretched between the top and bottom lashes.

"This has gone too far, Donnell. You look horrible – I-I can't even see you but something isn't right. And the smell..."

"I'm sorry," his voice cracked as another tear streamed down the part of his face that I could see. "I'm sorry for everything."

He tilted his head back slightly as the tears fell and the scabs around his mouth had advanced horribly, painfully; one side of his mouth appeared to be sealed beneath an over-growth of the sores.

"Let me see you. Please. You need help. Let me help you," I begged.

"You can't help me. Not anymore. It's too late."

He stuck his hand through the door and the sight of his swollen fingers squeez-ing through the crack made me gasp. The fin-gers were engorged the size of the packaged bratwurst sausages he liked to buy and put on the grill. They seem to be infused into each other so that they each moved together as he wiggled them as if to show me what he meant by *it's too late*. The nail beds had flattened and blended into the fingertips and the skin looked as if it were stretched taut from pressure.

From the looks of that mutated hand, it was indeed too late. He grunted and pulled back the hand, then leaned closer to the door opening, speaking to me with that eye.

"Don't come back down here again."

"I'm worried about you, please!"

"It'll be okay soon. Trust me," he said and began hacking up a vicious cough that made me take a step away from the opening. "It's gonna be okay." He growled again, but his eye said that he was terrified.

Suddenly, the door slammed shut and I heard the same sliding and dragging sound, until the squeak of the mattress spring.

My mind conquered up an image that sent a chill through my bones. Sobbing, I turned and ran upstairs to the relative safety of what used to be *our* bedroom.

———ele———

The bed was so cold without Donnell beside me.

I used to enjoy stretching out on the king-sized mattress on the nights when he would work late. But the difference was that I could feel the warmth in the spots where he had slept and the slight indentation of his body, and smell his scent on his pillow. It had been so long since Donnell had slept next to me that the bed no longer felt like I'd ever shared it with another soul.

I missed his presence in the house. He was there, but yet, he wasn't. He was just downstairs, the guest room was beneath our bedroom so he still felt as if he were there but yet, he wasn't. At night when it was quiet, I could hear his ragged breathing wafting up through the ceiling and into my ears as I lay in bed. In fact, I turned off the television at night just so I could hear him beneath me. Knowing he was there comforted me just a little bit.

Weeks before – before things got so terribly bad, he'd lost his job and I know that did a number on his self-esteem. When he used to rise early, hum songs under his breath as he got dressed and headed out before the sun could rise, now he didn't even start sliding around until at least noon. The mattress would squeak, he'd slide across the floor, bumping into furniture; toilet flushing, more sliding and bumping and the squeaking of springs when he returned to the sleeper sofa.

I don't know exactly when the shift happened but days would go by and he wouldn't even come out of the room. There were only so many sick days he could have taken until he'd have to apply for short term disability, and in order to do that, he'd have to have a doctor's approval, which meant, well, he'd have to leave the room.

The cat was ripped out of the bag on the day I got a phone call from Ralph, the owner of the restaurant Donnell had managed for nearly 10 years. After Donnell failed to show up at work for a full week, Ralph had no choice but to terminate his position. He finally reached out to me to get a message to Donnell about picking up his personal items.

I nervously walked into the restaurant and immediately felt self-conscious due to all of the eyes I imagined were staring at me.

That's his wife.

Who, her? For real?

That's her!

At least, that's what I thought I heard as I made my way to the hostess stand where I was greeted by a blonde girl named Timothee, according to her name tag.

She smiled big and wide, so wide that I wondered if she knew me before I introduced myself.

"I'm here to pick up some things for Donnell Witten," I said, trying to match her energy.

"Donnell? Are you his...wife?" Timothee asked, lowering her voice on *wife*.

I cleared my throat and straightened my back, not sure why, but I felt like I needed to stand taller.

"Yes, I'm his wife. Ralph called me to stop by," I replied.

"Of course, yes, give me just a moment to grab everything," Timothee's smile dimmed a little bit as she turned to disappear into the hall leading to the restaurant offices.

While I waited, a small table next to the hostess stand drew my attention. The framed photograph of a gorgeous brown-skinned woman sporting a short bob was surrounded by small unlit candles and a potted plant. A small number of cards in envelopes, assumed condolences, were neatly stacked next to a donation jar that was filled to the top with cash.

Timothee returned and stood quietly behind me as I leaned over to read the handwritten words on the small placard.

"That's Sophia. She died about a month ago," said Timothee, reaching around me to straighten the items on the table and wipe at a fleck of imaginary dust on Sophia's picture.

"I'm sorry for your loss. I can tell she was well loved," I kept a straight face and a friendly smile, but my thoughts were screaming so loudly that I was afraid Timothee could hear them.

"The customers wanted to do something for her kids. We *all* loved her. She didn't deserve this."

I refrained from asking, *didn't deserve what, exactly?* Not only because it might be rude but also because deep inside, I already had my suspicions about the *what*.

A young man approached holding a Sterlite container between both hands. He stood next to me and joined us staring at Sophia's memoriam, until I broke the spell by nodding toward the plastic container.

"Mine?"

He nodded in return. "Heavy."

A group of customers entered so Timothee smiled at me and scooted back to her station. I was ready to leave anyway so I was grateful for the distraction. The young man followed me to my car and placed Donnell's property on the back seat while I held the door open for him. After he disappeared back inside of the restaurant, I climbed into the back seat and closed the door, pulling the plastic tub onto my lap.

When I removed the lid, I realized that it smelled like him. His scent wafted up to my nose, my face, and filled the car, and I liked it because it smelled like the old Donnell, the one I used to love. His cologne, Nautica, and the scent of his dried sweat in the folded hoodie, gloves and wool cap. I held the cap to my nose and inhaled deeply and it was comforting.

The other items in the container were mostly non-essential, a coffee cup, some business books and sports magazines, a pack of cigarettes (apparently, he smoked at work too) and an unopened box of condoms. Well, those was pretty essential. I took no comfort in the fact that he didn't have the decency to even open the box much less use them.

Before closing the container, I decided to flip through the books and almost immediately a photo tumbled from the pages to the car seat. I knew what I would see even before I picked it up and flipped it over.

The entire staff posed together at the front of the dining room. They looked so happy! I could tell they were a close-knit group, unlike the hapless band of idiots that Donnell often made them out to be. I spotted both Timothee and the kid who had carried the bin to my car, and in the back was Donnell standing shoulder to shoulder with Not-Fat Sophia from the framed photograph.

At first glance, the group photo seemed harmless, just a friendly gathering of coworkers posing for a picture. But as I held it up to the light and examined it closely, I found exactly what I was searching for. My gaze followed Donnell's arm behind the person in front of him, down to where his hand intertwined with Sophia's in the small gap between their bodies.

_____ *ell* _____

I dreamed of him again, except I didn't know it was a dream. I had been lying in the dark and quiet bedroom, listening to him moving around downstairs, moaning plaintively like one of those sad whales in the science documentaries.

Wooon.

Wooon.

Suddenly, the bed shifted beneath his weight and before I could roll over to look at him, I felt hands sliding up my back and beneath my arms. Up, up they went, across my breasts, teasing my nipples into hardness, then tickling the sides of my throat with the tips of his fingers and pressing the palm of his hand firmly into the base of my neck.

He pulled me over and kissed the lids of my eyes, probing for entry between my thighs which parted easily at his touch.

By the time my hips began to rise and meet his deep strokes, my head was already pounding with the roar of blood trapped between his fists. My oxygen was cut off and my brain was screamed for air but something inside my center was screaming for more him. My legs rose to wrap around his waist and pull him in tighter, but I was confused at having to choose between the beautiful assault of my deepest core and the darkness sitting at the edge of my brain, waiting for me to tap out.

Instinctively, my hands flew up to grip his forearms; squeezing and tearing into his skin with my fingernails. His hands left my throat and I gasped for air, climaxing with a force that shook my thighs and made them tremble around his waist. The air returning to my lungs felt like icicles tumbling down my throat, slicing flesh along the way, surely destroying everything in its path beyond my tongue.

"Come with me," He sobbed into the base of my neck. "Please. Tika, I'm scared!" His tears were cold; they fell on my skin and rolled down to the sheets. The shock of dampness woke me up from the dream where I found myself shivering from sweat that pooled on my neck and cold air coming through the open window.

I did something different after that dream. I got up and locked the bedroom door before going back to sleep.

— ℓℓℓ —

During in the summer, warm breezes would blow the odor from our house into the neighbor's yard and although she never came to my door to ask, I could tell she was curious by her facial expressions when I'd see her in passing. Having open windows was no longer possible once the cold weather set in, I had to resort to wearing my outdoor clothing indoors. Bulky sweaters, hoodies, fleece-lined hoodies and chunky socks while I moved around the house trying to keep warm.

I went into our savings and purchased half a dozen heavy duty air purifiers to place around the house and that seemed to do the trick. Mostly. There was this strange layer of rot just beneath the disinfected surface. Sort of like how the most rancid garbage leaves its memory in the air long after you've removed it from inside. No matter how much I scrubbed and sprayed, there was still something in the air that even the most industrial of filters couldn't banish.

"Donnell, honey?" I leaned my forehead against the door and it felt ice cold to the touch. I knew then that he was gone.

"Don?"

While I used a bobby pin to work the lock free, Donnell didn't protest nor did he move or bump or slide across the floor. I continued jiggling the pin in the lock but the sadness was already setting into the corners of my mouth.

Click.

The doorknob turned easily in my hand and I steeled myself for what I would see but a part of me wanted to leave him and his secrets alone. Just burn the house down around him so no one would ever have to know.

I pushed open the door and stepped into the frigid room. Everything was in complete disarray, as if someone or something had rushed through, knocking everything over

Something that used to be Donnell was lying on the bed. It wasn't Donnell. It didn't even seem human.

At first, I thought it was a pile of laundry and I stood contemplating whether I should be straightening up, setting the chairs and tables upright, collecting the plates and glasses stacked around the room. But I didn't pick the lock to do chores.

Steeling myself for what I already knew, I forced my feet to move closer to the bed. Squinting but I could barely make out the outline of Donnell's misshapen head against the pillow. His body – now a bloated unstructured shape made of skin – had spread across and sunk down into the mattress and I couldn't tell where he began nor ended. His facial features were almost completely melted away but I could still see a vague outline of where his eyes used to be, the indentation of his nose, and his mouth gaped open in the last moments of fear as death finally – gratefully – completed.

He'd spent the last few weeks of his life transforming into whatever this was, and while it made me a little sad, I was also angry because it was all his fault to begin with.

Still, I mourned for the man he used to be, not the man he was because I didn't know him. I mourned Donnell with the big toothy smile, the quick wit and the one-liners that had me in tears just moments after we met. I mourned the loss of his big brown eyes that could convince me to do just about anything, and did.

A nearly empty pack of cigarettes lay on the bedside table. The pack was full and I chuckled to myself as I thought about him waiting until his mouth had melted away before he finally kicked the habit. The old Donnell would have appreciated that joke at his expense. I fished around in the drawer until I found a lighter with just enough fluid to light the last cigarette.

I took two pulls and got a nice burn going on the tip, then I pressed it into the driest spot of the mattress and waited for it to catch and burn. As the smoke started to rise from the fire, I ran to the kitchen to grab my car keys and my purse, along with the folder of documents from the credenza in the hallway.

My neighbor was standing in her front yard looking at the smoke billowing out of my windows, her cellphone to her ear. I took a seat on the curb and waved at her smiling.

"Are you okay?" She asked as she rushed over to me with her arms outstretched.

The side of my stomach started to itch and I slipped my hand underneath my shirt to scratch; my fingers came away sticky with blood and bits of dead skin.

I shook my head and laughed as I let her pull me up from the curb. But my eyes would say that I was terrified.

Groundhog

FUCKING LIARS.

    With one, she shared a mother; with the other, she shared a bed. But they betrayed her in the worst possible way – and they would pay, oh, yes, they would pay.

    Smile at me, go ahead and ask me about my day as you try to throw me off the scent. But I can smell the guilt and deceit coming out of your pores – or should I say – between your filthy legs!

    My loving husband: come and kiss me on my cheek like you're happy to see me. I've trembled a thousand times under your hands on my body but tonight you will tremble under mine.

    My dear sister: pick up your eyes from the floor – my face is up here! That's right, you ARE a fledgling actress, but tonight will be your final curtain call.

    Alana paused at the mirror in the foyer to give them time to adjust their clothing. She frowned and plucked two crisp dead leaves from her blonde-tipped locs, adding them to the pile on the small table beneath the mirror.

"What would you guys like for dinner?" She asked, kicking off her pumps.

Keyon's eyes moved nervously between Alana's stockinged feet and the deepening red stains in the carpet by the chair.

"Whatever you decide is fine, Constance mumbled without looking up from the pages of a magazine she'd selected from the sofa table.

"Chicken it is." Alana breezed through the kitchen and into the garage where she peeled away a small pill case taped beneath the fuse box. Humming softly, she began preparing the meal. *Never let them see you sweat!* After fixing the plates, she turned her back to the living room and crushed a small white capsule into the potatoes on each of their plates.

She'd considered many ways to make them pay for their crime, from disabling the furnace to ensure a carbon monoxide leak, to triggering a house explosion, both of which would be perfect scenarios since she herself would be out of town. But ultimately, her profession provided her with the perfect weapon of destruction in the form of a convenient little pill. – cyanide. She'd dispose of the bodies and then make the "discovery" that the two had simply ran off together. *Never fuck with a chemist.*

"Dinner's ready," she called out sweetly, taking her seat at the end of the dining table so she could watch them devour their last meal.

The treacherous pair shuffled over and took their usual seats at the table.

"I need your share of the rent today, sis," Alana said, narrowing her eyes at Constance as she took a bite of her food. "Yesterday was the first."

"I got it, don't worry – you'll get it," Constance sighed and rolled her eyes.

Stay calm, it'll be over soon. "By the way, I have to drive some drug samples to Ohio after dinner. I missed the courier so I'll do it myself – will you two be okay here while I'm away?" *Of course, you will.*

Keyon cleared his throat. "Well, I mean, I guess – we'll manage, we always do."

You always do IT, you mean!

"I've got some lines to rehearse any-way," replied Constance, shooting Keyon a side glance that was unmistakably full of secrets. Alana cringed and resisted the urge to leap across the table.

"I need hot sauce," Keyon said around a mouthful of chicken.

The legs of his chair scraped loudly across the floor as Keyon pushed away from the table and passed behind Alana on his way to the kitchen. She opened her mouth to fuss about the scuff marks when Constance suddenly turned sideways and slammed her hand on the table.

"Do it! Do it!" Constance screamed, pounding the table with her fist.

Alana heard the *swish* of rough fabric and caught the quick flash of the belt as it dropped past her face and tightened against her neck. Fear and confusion took over as Constance taunted her and she struggled to understand what was taking place. Keyon pushed his knee into the back of her chair and pulled harder until he felt a soft pop; Alana's body went limp.

Constance jumped out of her chair and leaned her weight on her elbows to stare at her sister's lifeless body crumpled on the floor.

"That's your rent, bitch!" she spat vehemently. She looked up at Keyon and forced a reassuring smile. "Don't look so worried – we're safe now. Let's get rid of her and start practicing our alibis so you can report her missing."

Together, they carried Alana to the backyard and tossed her into the hole dug earlier. Keyon emptied a carton of lime over her body to mask the scent of death and they both shoveled dirt back into the hole until she was covered.

Out of breath, they returned to the house and devoured the dinner lovingly prepared by Alana. Murder had a way of revving up the appetite.

"One thing I'll miss about her – she sure could cook!" Keyon mumbled over a hearty belch and dropped his fork loudly onto the empty plate just as his throat began to close.

"I can cook just as good as—." Constance stopped mid-sentence and clawed at her stomach as she fell out of her chair, spewing the bloody contents of her stomach across the carpet.

The lovers locked eyes as they lay convulsing on the floor until death thankfully ended their torture.

Alana stumbled barefoot around the side of the house and into the front door. *Fucking liars,* she thought as she stopped to look at herself in the mirror. She picked a dry leaf from her locs and laid it on the foyer table before entering the living room to greet her disloyal family.

"What would you guys like for dinner?" She asked, kicking off her heels at the door.

"Whatever you choose," replied Constance, using the tip of her shoe to dab curiously at a red stain in the carpet.

Pins and Needles

PHILANA'S MORNINGS WERE ALWAYS the same: wake up to the pale light of dawn, cook a meager breakfast for herself and Noel, wash the dishes and do a load of laundry before heading off to work. It was a routine she had grown accustomed to, but one that offered little joy or satisfaction.

As she stared out the kitchen window, her hands scrubbing at a particularly stubborn stain on a plate, she realized how much that plate represented her soul, and that ugly stain – well, that would be Noel. Three years of marriage and she felt like all the life had been sucked out of her.

She worked a full-time job so the dishes and laundry were endless, the house was always a mess, and Noel did nothing but criticize and complain and crawl on top of her. Her entire existence had been whittled down to becoming his servant and sex slave

She felt fat and miserable and now he hadn't touched her in months except to push past her in the cramped hallway of their cramped apartment. Stuck in hell, she was, and she'd built it for herself brick by brick and sealed it with her own blood, sweat and tears.

As she finished washing the last dish, she looked up at the clock. It was time to leave for work. She sighed and dried her hands, then grabbed her coat and bag before heading for the door, but Noel stepped into the kitchen just as she touched the door handle.

"What about the baby?" He asked, looking at her with wide eyed disbelief.

She stopped and turned around to face him.

"What do you mean – you're home today, you can watch her!"

"Are you serious? My one day off and you think I wanna babysit?"

"You're not babysitting, Noel. She's YOUR child. And you hardly ever see her as it is. I figured she would like spending the day with you," Philana argued but she already knew how it would end. She began mentally preparing the message to her job to let them know she would be late.

"I'm not babysitting today. It's my one day off. I got shit to do. Take her to your mom's house."

"That'll make me late for work! You should have said something before now! You knew I had to work."

"And you knew I wasn't gonna watch no baby on my one day off. Didn't think that had to be said," Noel reached into the kitchen drawer and pulled out his drawstring bag and she knew the conversation was over. He lit a joint and walked past her and opened the back door to sit on the porch and smoke. He'd said what he said and that was the law.

Fighting tears, she typed a quick text message to Lia, the supervisor at the call center, informing her that she'd just stepped outside and discovered a flat tire. Since her husband had already left for work, she'd have to wait on roadside to come and fix it. That would buy her enough time to pack up the baby and drive a half hour away to her mother's house before heading to work.

Upsetting her plans and making her late for work was routine for Noel, and despite the tears now falling down her cheeks, she stayed ready to pivot. Honestly, she preferred taking the baby to her mother's anyway, since Noel's method of "babysitting" meant stuffing her with snacks until she puked and leaving the mess for Philana to clean up after working all day.

As she packed the diaper bag, an idea came to mind. She hadn't visited Noel's mother in over a year. Maybe it was time for a trip out to the old farmhouse. She had no doubt that Noel would love it if she left him with an empty house for the weekend. In fact, it would please him the most but it would also give her a bit of peace from his controlling eye.

His mother Mirelles was odd, preferring the company of her cats and herbs to people. But she had mostly always been kind to Philana. *Mostly.* After they got past the initial rough patch. But she seemed to possess some sort of secret wisdom, as if she could see right through a person to their soul. Mirelles might understand better than anyone what Philana was going through.

The next day, Philana was bumping down the long dirt driveway, remembering the first time she came here when Noel brought her to meet his mother. She still felt nervous when she was in the woman's presence; her hands trembled a little as she parked the car and reflected on their early relationship. It had been uncomfortable at times, downright non-existent at others with small bright spots peeking out here and there.

It was no secret that Mirelles didn't quite approve of her joining the family. Philana still felt her nerves clinch when she remembered the day that she and Noel happily announced their engagement to Mirelles. Visibly bothered, the old woman sucked her teeth and mumbled a terse, 'congratulations,' and maintained a cold, toothy grin for the remainder of dinner. As soon as Noel left the room to go to the bathroom, Mirelles leaned toward Philana's shoulder and whispered, "You won't make it, girl. He needs someone to tell him 'No' and I can already tell you're the type to let him walk all over you."

Philana froze, unable to respond; her lips quivered as she fought the urge to break down and cry.

"He's like his daddy. He'll eat you alive and spit you out, if you let him. I'll pray for your soul."

Footsteps in the hall signaled Noel's return, to Philana's great relief. Mirelles slipped back to her seat and sat glaring at her over the rim of her coffee cup.

He'll eat you alive.

Those words played over and over in Philana's head through the years. Especially as things grew worse and she realized too late that she had made a huge mistake in marrying Noel. How often she wished that when Mirelles whispered her fate into her ear, she should have gotten into her car and driven far away, never looking back.

Mirelles opened the creaky screen door before Philana knocked. She rushed out onto the porch and started smothering Baby Erme in kisses, exclaiming. "Oh my, look at my grandbaby! I've missed you so!"

She greeted Philana with an affectionate touch on her elbow and a direct look into her eyes as she took the baby from her arms.

"Come out of the cold!"

The inside of the house smelled of dried herbs and tea tree oil, probably from the flowers hanging from the ceiling perfuming the air. The mantle over the fireplace was lined with every shape and size of glittering crystals, next a tall shelf of leather-bound vintage-looking books that Philana suspected were full of incantations and spells. One row of the shelf was filled with ornately-decorated wooden antique boxes that Philana always found intriguing, as Noel hinted that she'd collected them since before he was born.

The house vibrated with an energy that made her feel both welcomed and wary. Clearly the discomfort was only sensed by Philana, but it was so distinct that it made the hairs on her arms stand up.

Mirelles led Philana to the kitchen table and sat across from her, bouncing the baby on her lap.

"You look a mess," she said, her dark eyes peering intently at Philana as she planted a kiss on top of baby Erme's curly head. "And you've thickened up since I last saw you. What's going on, chile?"

Haltingly at first, then with increasing emotion, Philana described her marriage and how lifeless she felt. Mirelles listened silently, nodding and occasionally cooing toward Erme as she started to fall asleep on her lap.

"I see," she said when Philana finished. "You feel trapped. But there are always options, if only we open our eyes."

She stood abruptly and handed the sleeping baby to Philana. "Wait here. I have something that might help."

Philana watched curiously as Mirelles shuffled over to the shelf and began sorting through the decorative boxes. She was a small, frail woman who gave off an elderly aura but she was only in her sixties. The legend that preceded her added to her mystery. Noel often called her a witch, but Philana never knew if he was being sarcastic or if he really believed his mother had magical powers. Mirelles didn't hide the fact that she dabbled in darkness, that was well known throughout the family, but whether or not she was effective, that was the question. She had lost two babies after Noel, and then her husband – Noel's father – had disappeared. Philana felt that Mirelles kept that veneer of steel to hide that kind of deep-rooted sadness, and it's the only reason she continued to give grace to the old mean lady.

She came back to the table a few minutes later clutching something small, wrapped in black velvet. She stood in front of Philana and said, "Open your hand."

Philana obeyed, and Mirelles dropped the smooth bundle of fabric onto her fingers. She pressed around the shape of something enclosed in the velvet, and she peeled back the flaps to find a simple, ragged doll-like cushion with a tiny red heart sewn on its chest and a button for its eye. The dull, stained fabric and crude stitching along the edges spoke to its age, if she had to guess, several decades old.

But it was hauntingly beautiful, and ostensibly sad and disturbing.

She traced her finger along the leg.

"Be careful!" Mirelles reached out and pressed along the foot, then slowly pulled out a straight pin with a gold-tipped head; she dropped it onto the velvet cloth.

"Is this...what I think it is?" Philana whispered, reaching over Erme's head to lay the doll on the table.

Mirelles placed her hand protectively over the top of it and it was small enough that it hid completely beneath her palm.

"I made this the day he was born." She said quietly.

"Who?"

"Your husband. My son." She raised her hand and tapped the red heart on the doll's chest. "A part of him is in there. I knew I would need protection one day and I wanted to be prepared."

Philana was flabbergasted. From watching movies and reading books, she was somewhat familiar with voodoo dolls and their purpose, but she never expected to learn that her own husband had a voodoo doll in his likeness.

She felt her anger rise but she knew better than to allow it to show on her face. Her husband may be a misogynistic, narcissistic bully, but...a voodoo doll? It wasn't that serious! Swallowing hard, Philana tried to calmly voice her concern.

"Mom. Why on earth would you need something like that for your son – for your baby?"

Mirelles chuckled. "I told you years ago, he's like his father. You might think you know him, but you don't. I do." She reached out to stroke Erme's chunky arm as she continued sleeping.

"How do you even make such a thing?"

"A few days after he was born, I clipped his fingernails with those little tiny baby nail clippers, and I put the nails in here," Mirelles stroked the red heart on the doll's chest.

Philana shivered. "I just can't believe it. I would never do such a thing."

"Of course, you wouldn't. And that's why you're here. Asking me for help. Look, I'm not giving you this to kill him. That's my son and I love him. But I also know you need to protect yourself and them babies from him."

"Protect us from what exactly?" Philana asked.

Mirelles gave her a blank stare, as if she knew the answer to the question.

"Look, I just needed to vent to you, Mom. I don't know how we ended up down this road. I'm not afraid of my husband. I just want him to be a better husband and father. I'm not trying to get rid of him!"

"Then learn how to take away some of his power." Mirelles pushed the doll back into Philana's hand. "I told you years ago that he would eat you alive. This is your shield against his teeth, so to speak."

Although she thought Mirelles was batshit crazy, Philana replaced the pin in the doll's foot, wrapped it carefully in the velvet and dropped it into her bag. This wasn't what she came there for. She expected words of wisdom, not witchcraft. *But that's what you get when you go to a witch.* Shaking her head, she rocked Erme softly in her arms, hearing Mirelles' words repeat in her head. *This is your shield against his teeth.*

Mirelles was asleep in her bed when Noel violently kicked open the front door and began running up the stairs to her bedroom. He hit the light switch on the wall with a heavy hand, and began shaking his fists and screaming at the top of his lungs. Groggy and confused, she bolted straight up in the bed.

"YOU GAVE THIS TO MY WIFE? ARE YOU TRYING TO KILL ME?" He raged and swung his arm in the air, pitching something across the room. It hit her in the face and fell down to the blanket; the velvet cloth came apart and the crudely sewn doll spilled out.

Mirelles braced herself for his anger as she picked up the doll and turned it around in her hand. She felt the leg for the presence of the pin. It was there. Sighing, she tried to calm herself before speaking in an even toned voice.

"Noel, let me explain."

"Explain? EXPLAIN? How do you explain *that*?"

"You're right. I actually can't explain it. But what I can say is that I was only trying to help-"

"Help my wife kill me?"

"No-no-no-no. That's not what we discussed at all. You know...you know what I do. Don't act as if you don't." As she spoke, she kept her forefingers braced on the legs of the doll.

"How about we ask *her* what you were trying to do?" Noel said menacingly. As if on cue, Philana stepped into the room from behind his back.

"Hi, Mom," she said, smiling meekly, but her eyes were sad and red from crying.

She kept her eyes down, looking at the floor, ashamed.

"Where's the baby? Where's the baby?"

"She's with the sitter!" Philana replied as Noel pushed her into the center of the room. Mirelles glared at her, but she refused to look up and meet her eyes.

"She said you told her to leave me – ain't that right, honey? Ain't that what she said?"

"Yes," Philana replied softly.

"And the doll, what was the doll for?"

"The doll was for her protection," Mirelles spoke up, sliding her legs out of the bed to stand. Her heart was racing but she wouldn't let him see her falter, after all, she had prepared 32 years for this fight.

"YOU'RE INSANE. THIS IS EXACTLY WHY DAD LEFT! HE DIDN'T LEAVE ME, HE WANTED TO GET AWAY FROM YOU!" Noel screamed, angrily, spit flying from his mouth.

Mirelles shook her head, her eyes pleaded with Noel.

"If you only knew what I saw that night, that night he-he...disappeared. If you only knew-"

"Tell me then! You keep saying that but you never tell me – what did you see?"

"My babies! They didn't deserve what he did to them, but there was something in his bones that he couldn't fight," sobbed Mirelles. "And I saw that same hunger deep inside your eyes the day you were born. I felt it when I held you to my breast, my milk wouldn't be enough to satisfy you."

"What are you talking about, you crazy old lady!" Noel's nostrils flared and he bared his teeth at his mother.

Mirelles stood her ground and stared back at him even as he towered over her.

"I know what you are. You're just like your father," she said, boldly, refusing to look away. "You don't scare me."

Growing angrier at the fact that he couldn't shake her, he turned and stormed out of the room.

"Where are the rest of them, huh? I know you've got more in this house! I'm gonna find them and put a stop to this!"

Mirelles turned her gaze to Philana, standing nervously by the doorway.

"You foolish girl! I tried to protect you and you betray me like this?" Mirelles hissed at her.

"Shut up, old woman! Just shut up! You're the one making voodoo dolls. Why can't you save yourself? Aren't you supposed to be a witch?" Philana whispered back at her. "Do something about him!"

"That's for YOU to do now. He's YOUR husband."

Noel stomped back into the room, holding an arm full of the voodoo dolls made of various fabrics, colors, and adornments. He dumped them on the bed and sorted through them.

"So, this is what you've been doing? Controlling people with these – these dolls? What's this one? Why does it look like Dad? You made this for him? DID YOU GET RID OF HIM TOO?"

Mirelles pressed her lips together, refusing to answer.

"Okay, I see, I get it," Noel nodded, backing away. "You'll never see us again."

"And I'm taking these," He scooped up the dolls and headed for the door. "Come on, Philana!"

She followed meekly behind him. Now alone, Mirelles collapsed on the bed. There was nothing else she could do for Philana.

"He's gonna eat her alive." She said, and whimpered softly to herself.

"Open the window and toss those gross things out," Noel demanded as he sped toward home.

Philana did as she was told, rolling down her window and flinging the entire bundle of dolls into the night. She briefly wondered if someone might stumble upon them and take them home, clean them up, put them in a yard sale. Or, a squirrel picks it apart for the cotton inside and uses it to stuff its hideout.

Perhaps they should have kept them and stored them safely away. She shrugged. *Too late now.*

Noel was silent for the rest of the ride. Philana lost herself in her thoughts; she felt sad that Mirelles was now being cut from her life too. She felt ashamed that she wasn't able to stand up to Noel and keep the secret that Mirelles had entrusted her with, but Mirelles should have known better than to give her that kind of responsibility. She *knew* she wasn't strong! What did she tell her? *He's gonna eat you alive.* So, it was really her fault for trusting her with the doll! She should have kept it herself and pushed the pins in it. Now all the dolls were gone forever. She idly wondered if Mirelles would get the chance to make more.

Arriving home, Noel went to free the sitter while Philana headed for the bedroom.

Her mind was racing with anxiety over the evening's events. She took a hot shower and tried to relax but Mirelles haunted her thoughts. Noel had not come to join her in the bedroom and she needed to get a better handle on his state of mind, because that would determine her level of comfort for the next few days.

She stepped into the hallway and caught a glimpse of him exiting the baby's room.

"Noel. Noel!" She called out but he quickly turned away from her and headed down the stairs. Confused, she followed behind until she caught up with him in the kitchen.

"Noel! Didn't you hear me-"

As she drew closer, Noel abruptly came to a halt and spun around to confront her. His mouth and neck were covered with blood, presumably the same blood that soaked the front of his shirt. Philana halted, her mind a jumble of memories and scenes and words that never made sense before, but now it all made perfect sense.

"He'll eat you alive."

She never even had a chance to scream before he ripped into her.

Labor Pains

GEORGE WOODBRIDGE WASN'T A very bright man, but one thing he knew he could do was deliver babies.

He'd read books on pregnancy and childbirth, and watched countless YouTube videos of women giving birth, but securing the janitor's position at the hospital provided him with unlimited access to medical supplies. Completely under the radar, George smuggled drugs and surgical instruments out of the hospital in his lunchbox and often, under his jacket, and none were the wiser.

In his small cottage-styled home on a quiet suburban street, he had been using his internet education and the stolen tools to deliver babies in secret for several years. The birth of Angel presented him with the first opportunity to put his skills to the test, and he delivered her safely and without issue, however, Brittany's high-risk delivery was challenging and almost made him doubt his abilities. By the time the twins Charlie and Danyelle came screaming into the world, his self-confidence was restored once he hugged their warm slippery bodies to his chest.

But each successful delivery pushed him closer and closer to the brink of madness.

"Don't push until I tell you to," George ordered, wiping the sweat from his brow as he spoke soothingly to the woman laboring on the bed. "It's going beautifully; you're doing great, honey."

She groaned through her teeth and gripped the bed rails so tightly that her fingernails cut in her palms and drew blood. "Please, please, please, I need to push!" The pain from the contractions subsided as the baby's head squeezed into her lower section. After 14 long hours in labor, the urge to push had become overwhelming but she chewed on her bottom lip and suppressed her cries.

"Okay, I can see the head now – that's a lot of hair," he joked. "We're almost there, sweetheart!"

They had done this many times before, so she trusted him to safely guide her through; she pushed at his command and expelled the baby from her body with relative ease. Collapsing on her back so she could catch her breath, she kept her ear trained in his direction so she could gauge his reaction. In the moments that followed, her brief excitement at the delivery was replaced by dread and fear of the silence that hung thick in the air while George examined the newborn.

"George?

She could hear the baby softly whimpering but George's silence was deafening. Eventually, he uttered an anguished moan and she heard the rubber soles of his boots strike the floor as he stepped away from her. Tears welled up in her eyes as she squeezed them shut and opened her mouth and wailed.

The baby sputtered and coughed as George wrapped it tightly in a flannel receiving blanket and turned to leave the basement, holding it in the crook of his arm like a quarterback on his way to score the winning touchdown.

"Wait, please – can I see her first?" The woman begged weakly, searching for a hint of compassion in his stern face. He deliberately looked in the opposite direction as he passed, holding the baby away from her, ignoring her pleas. He mounted the basement stairs and slipped out the side door, heading to the shed behind the house.

The long walk down the path to the secret place; retrieving from beneath the cabinet a roll of hazardous waste bags and medical tape; the slow drawing of water into the tub - it was a ritual with which he was all too familiar. Placing the baby on the table next to the tub, he reached into the overhead cabinet and withdrew the small rubber plugs for his ears, heavy duty leather gloves that reached to his elbows. After draping himself in the thick plastic vest, he pushed the plugs into his ears and donned the gloves before opening the blanket. He scooped the baby with both hands and laid her, naked and wiggling, into the cold plastic tub.

His rough hands smoothed the infant's silky black hair as he examined her. Her face was tiny, round, with creamy terra cotta skin still adjusting its tone to the air and light. He tried not to show revulsion at her deformity; he didn't want such an expression to be the last image she saw, as if it really mattered in the grand scheme of things. She stared back at him with wide trusting eyes and he kept his lips pressed together in a tight half smile, avoiding her gaze. Her little feet kicked harmlessly against his stomach and made tiny squeaking sounds as they brushed against the protective covering.

"You're the sixth, so I'm going to call you Farrah," He whispered, using his fingers to drizzle water across her cheeks. Baby Farrah squealed as the wet droplets rolled down her cheeks into the opening of her ear.

Her tiny fingers found his wrist and she grasped wildly at his arms for balance as he lowered her into the tub. As the water rose around her head and covered her ears, the one-inch wide slit in the center of her fore-head popped open and the eye glared at him accusingly. Her mouth gaped and emitted a high-pitched wail that filled the tiny shed and pierced George's eardrums.

George snatched one hand away from her grasp and suffered a deep cut on the back of his hand as her claws cut into his flesh. The third eye blinked at him furiously as Baby Far-rah whipped her head from side to side and tried to nip at his hand with her tiny mouth. She caught the edge of his finger and he could feel a row of sharp fangs bear down on the glove before he snatched away.

He pressed her head to the bottom of the tub and held her still, looking away until she gave up the struggle. Her muffled underwater screams created bubbles that rose to the surface and obscured her monstrous face.

Baby Farrah was going to haunt his dreams for a long time; much longer than the others. Each baby's transformation was more demonic and terrifying than the previous; and the subsequent nightmares grew darker and more hopeless as time passed. Each time George made the walk to the shed, he feared that it might be him that wouldn't emerge.

———*ele*———

"George, we have to try again. As soon as she heals."

His wife Leolah sat calmly in the kitchen at the top of the basement stairs. She normally stayed far away during the deliveries and waited instead for George to walk down the hallway to their bedroom where she waited nervously for him to present her with a perfectly, healthy baby. A human baby.

But Leolah was getting restless and impatient, and all of the failures were wearing on her soul. She stood in the kitchen this time, listening to the soft cries of the child and cringing at the sound of George's boots on the basement stairs. Her breath caught in her throat as she anticipated which way he would turn when he reached the top. Her heart sank when she heard him pull open the door to leave the house because then she knew.

She'd sat quietly and watched him exit the side door with the bundle beneath his arms; there was no need for questioning things for which she already knew the answers. She glared at him with a mixture of sadness and disgust, and picked up a pack of cigarettes from the table. Holding the cigarette between her lips, she leaned slightly forward, waiting for George to obediently pick up the lighter and set fire to the end of the cigarette.

"But after that, she has to go. Time to replace and refresh!" She said flippantly, as if she were instructing him to purchase new bathroom towels.

"Yes, honey," George agreed, staring down at his calloused fingers; the light from the kitchen window gave his mocha-colored hands a tint of copper, like sparks of magic in contrast to the horrible act he had just been forced to perform.

"I'm going to do another spell on her, while her womb is open. Gather my items and then bring her to me, said Leolah, dismissing him with a nod of her head.

George shuffled down the hallway into the bedroom and retrieved the doll from the drawer. With one arm, he held it stiffly against his chest as he rushed about the room, collecting the additional items he knew she would request next. He grabbed the three partially melted tapered candles and holders and a Ziploc bag of dried oak leaves, clutching them tightly between his fingers as he pinched the red wax marker from the bottom of the dresser drawer.

He headed to the living room and dutifully began the ritual which he knew by heart: arranging the candles in their holders in the shape of a triangle and lighting each one; then he stacked the leaves into a pile at her feet and set fire to the edges with his lighter. A tightly rolled yoga mat leaned against the coffee table; George grabbed it and snapped it open, spreading it on the floor at Leolah's feet. She pulled up the front of her muumuu and squatted, resting her hands on her bent knees. Her eyes were closed, head tilted to the ceiling, and her braids spilled down her back, giving her a regal appearance that reminded George of why he was so smitten with her when they met. She began breathing deeply, settling into her meditation pose, and George almost lost himself in his thoughts of how beautiful she was to him in that moment.

She rocked gently back and forth as she cradled the doll to her breasts, whispering wildly into the molded rubber ears on the side of the doll's head.

George laid the marker next to the pile of leaves and backed up until he ran into the wall on the far side of the room, where he stood and watched silently. He knew to stay far out of the way while she worked her spells, as it was often unpredictable, messy and even dangerous. But George assisted her with whatever she required because he knew that the black veil over their lives was because of him; it was punishment not only for their union but for that horrible thing he'd done several years earlier on that quiet Sunday morning, before the curse had been placed upon them.

The way he remembered, it seemed to have been someone else whose hand lingered a bit too long on the back of Baby George's head, pressing his face deep into the crib mattress. In his mind, he was floating above the room, watching it take place, and even though he screamed at the man in the room to stop, the figure ignored him and continued firmly patting and pressing, until Baby George struggled no more.

Now, all Leolah wanted was another baby, but in his own selfishness, all George wanted was her.

"Get her. NOW!" She barked impatiently, interrupting his thoughts. "The leaves burn quickly, there's no time to waste!"

——*ele*——

Her name was Lily.

Six years earlier, he'd found her at the truck stop over by the highway. She was cold, hungry and willing to do anything to avoid returning to an abusive pimp. George had something she could do. Suddenly he had the answer to his and Leolah's problem sitting in the passenger seat of his car. Lily was very similar to Leolah with her petite frame, tawny beige skin and full lips, so George saw their meeting as a sign. To Lily, the stranger's offer seemed like a no-brainer at the time, but she had no idea of the real horror she was agreeing to in exchange for housing.

It didn't take much to sell the idea to Leolah, after all, she wanted another baby more than anything in the world, even more than she wanted him. But they had been cursed and could produce nothing together, at least, nothing that could be considered a child.

He led Lily into the room where his wife sat cross-legged in the floor. The pile of oak leaves smoldered on the floor in front of her, and the three candles still burned in a triangle at her back. A faint stream of white smoke rose to the ceiling and Leolah waved her hand through the line to spread it into the air.

"Hurry up, lay her down on the mat!" Leolah barked, carefully placing the doll on the floor at her thigh.

Lily held on to George's arm and dutifully lowered herself to the rubber mat, carefully, grimacing at the pain between her legs from giving birth just hours earlier. Leolah pushed up the girl's t-shirt up to expose her stomach, and without another word, she used the red marker to scrawl tiny words on Lily's stomach.

"Sow in my womb a child as tall and healthy as the mighty oak."

She sat back and gazed at her handiwork before reaching behind for one of the tapered candles. Lily closed her eyes tightly and balled her fists, steeling herself for the pain to come.

Leolah read the phrase aloud three times while tilting the candle slightly to allow drops of wax to spill onto the girl's body.

She repeated the action with the two remaining candles, then scooped a handful of the burned leaves and scattered them through her fingers across Lily's belly.

Lily arched her back and accepted the dusting of the ashes; it felt somewhat soothing on top of the wax and it also signaled the end of Leolah's twisted ceremony. She knew she would soon return to the basement and await George's arrival in a few weeks to *seed* her, as Leolah liked to refer to it. But she'd have a welcomed break from him until that time came.

"I'm finished, take her back," Leolah picked up the doll and scooted around until her back was facing George and Lily.

George climbed the stairs slowly, rehearsing the words he would say when he faced Leolah. He had made that miserable trip up the stairs so many times with the same result, yet he still wasn't sure what he would say when their fortunes changed.

His hands were shaking when he reached out and gripped the banister to help steady his climb. He knew that once he reached the top of the stairs, their lives were about to change and not necessarily for the better. He imagined presenting Leolah with the baby and having to watch her melt down into an emotional mess once she realized that the curse was gone and her dream had finally come true. After which she would become obsessed over the child's every whimper, sniffle and sigh, and her entire existence would become entwined with her baby. She would spend night after night sitting next to his crib and staring at him under the moonlight shining through the window, stroking his fat cheeks with her fingers, leaning over to feel his breath on her cheek.

He remembered wryly how it was before. Leolah loved that baby so much that she didn't even know George was alive. All he could do was watch from afar; dare he even attempt to touch, soothe or pacify the child – HIS child – she would shriek and swoop down upon them as if she thought George was going to cause harm.

He reached the last step and his knees buckled, causing him to almost pitch forward and lose his grip on the child in his arms. He paused before turning the corner into the kitchen, listening for the sound of Leolah rocking back and forth in her chair in the bedroom, but he couldn't hear a sound and the silence caused him to panic. He took a deep breath and scaled the last big step, landing in the center of the doorway.

He was surprised to find that Leolah was missing from her usual spot at the kitchen table. The small round ashtray held a single cigarette that burned unattended. He could then hear her moving around and slamming drawers in their bedroom down the hall. It was a clear sign that he needed to seize upon that moment to make his move. He turned quickly on his heel and rushed out the side door and down the pathway toward the shed. His heart was pulsing in his ears as he feared Leolah would suddenly rush through the house and jump on his back as he moved further and further away from the house, gripping the baby between both of his hands. He made it to the shed and pushed inside, then slammed the door and locked it behind him.

"What should I call you, little guy?" George held the baby boy under the lamp on the bench and stared into his perfect face. The boy blinked – his two perfect eyes blinked and George smiled. He used his fingers to examine the baby's head and along the spine for horn-like formations. He cautiously pressed a fingertip against the forehead, seeking an opening but relieved when the skin failed to pop open and reveal an angry eye like each of the others. The baby opened his mouth to utter cries, newborn cries, not the screeches of a wounded mythical animal – and George noted with satisfaction the healthy pink gums, no sign of sharp fangs breaking through the tissue.

"I will call you...Geno. Baby Geno, nice to meet you," he said before lowering perfect Geno into the tub of water.

When he returned to the house, Leolah was sitting at the kitchen table, dragging deeply on a cigarette as she watched him with suspicious eyes. She waved a hand toward a hot cup of tea sitting at the empty chair, signaling him to take a seat.

He pulled the chair away from the table and sank his tired body into the seat. Nervousness caused his hands to tremble but he avoided Leolah's eyes and drank until the cup was empty. Heat flowed through his body and he felt instantly relaxed; he leaned his back against the chair and raised his heavy head to look at his wife.

"It wasn't me," Leolah said, narrowing her eyes as the smoke from her cigarette crossed her face.

"What?"

"It wasn't me. She didn't curse my womb. We had it all wrong. She cursed *you*," Leolah mimicked the voice of George's ex-wife. *"All of your babies will carry the scars of your betrayal and you will shake with fear when you gaze upon their faces."*

George shuddered and recalled the last time he'd seen his ex-wife and their children. The day that he packed his belongings while Leolah and newborn Baby George waited for him in the car; his kids were clinging to each other in tears, while his wife stood in the doorway, chanting and screaming threats at George and Leolah as they drove away to begin anew.

His eyelids wanted to close, he was so hot and tired, but he struggled to focus on Leolah's face and the words coming out of her mouth.

"I should have known, *sweet Judayo*, what was I thinking all of this time!" Leolah closed her eyes and shook her head slowly, side to side. "One priestess cannot curse another priestess, it doesn't work, it protects us from our own emotions."

"Wait...wha? Whaddya mean?" George stuttered, his arms felt like weights and they fell from the table to dangle on each side of the chair. His body felt inflamed as the heat rushed from the top of his head down through his groin, and the surface of his skin glowed a blazing red from the intensity.

"We've been doing it all wrong. I know that now."

George gasped for air and struggled to remain in the chair but he had lost all feeling in his limbs and he began to slide toward the floor. Leolah's face floated before his eyes and he felt as if he were being sucked into a fiery furnace, but he couldn't even raise his hands in defense.

"Time to replace and refresh," Leolah said, taking another drag from her cigarette as she watched her husband's lifeless body crumple to the floor and burst into flames.

Originally appeared as "The Surrogate", Freestyle Friday, 9/2017; also in Black Magic Women, 2018

Seed

AUTHOR'S NOTE: THIS IS a work of satire; however, the concept was developed based on real online communities that fetishize mixed babies. This is an exclusive sneak peek into my upcoming novella, Seed, slated for May 2025. Let me know what you think!

"Keep your head down and run. Don't stop until you cross the opening where the trees divide. If you hear anyone running behind you, don't turn around, don't look behind you, and most of all...don't stop. Even if you hear someone calling your name, DO...NOT...STOP!"

Mase dropped his eyes and looked at the shredded rubber around the toes of his shoes. He'd spent far too many hours crouching in a starting position, ready to bolt at the sound of approaching danger; he would need to find another pair before his toes burst through the top.

"Are you hearing me, Mase?" His sister whispered angrily and shook his shoulders. Her face inches away, a spray of saliva hit the boy's face as she pressed closer, trying urgently to reach him.

"I'm not kidding, don't stop for nothing!"

Mase shrugged away and wiped at his face with the sleeve. "I hear you. I got it."

He forced a reassuring smile but the corners of his mouth quivered and betrayed his tough facade. He knew Stori was only trying to keep him safe but he was growing weary of her smothering him. She treated him like a child, like her child and not her 16-year-old brother. She was always watching him, hovering nearby ready to swoop down like a hawk if she sensed even the slightest danger nearby. He was so over it. Soon he would demand that she back off because after all they had been through, he had more than proven that he was a man.

Stori threw her red locs over her shoulder with one hand and leaned in to plant a kiss on her brother's cheek.

"I love you, Mase, I'll see you in a few days - don't forget our signal so I'll know you made it."

"I know - five stones to the right of the door, got it. Love you too, sis."

He took a few steps away and stopped to button his jacket and adjust his clothing. Pulling the hood over his head, he tugged at the drawstrings and tied them beneath his chin. The lower pocket of his cargo pants held his paper identification, a folded list of surviving relatives and their last known addresses, and the dollar bills that Stori had given him. He patted his pocket protectively and smiled as he pictured himself walking into a corner store with money in his hand to purchase his favorite chips and soda. In better days.

"Go!" Stori hissed at him from behind.

"Slow down, baby...oh, yeah, just like that!"

Moira Beckwith lay on her back with her legs wrapped tightly around the man's waist, pulling him deeper inside as she gripped his ass with her hands. She used her palms to press him into her each time her hips rose to meet him; she strained to get all of him inside but he seemed to be holding back, he wasn't giving her every inch as the ad promised!

"I need more!" She screamed over his shoulder, removing her legs from his back and placing her feet on the bed so she could grind harder into him.

Her face twisted into an obscene grimace as she worked to pull the man deeper inside and used her hands to guide his hips. Visibly frustrated, she groaned through her clenched teeth and humped upward, trying to control the act but something wasn't lining up, something just wasn't clicking and she was getting angrier with each minute that passed.

The man kept pumping until he moaned and threw back his head as he began to climax.

"Noooooooo!" Moira screamed into his ear and struck him on his back with her fists. "Don't you dare come yet! I paid for the premium package! I demand you keep going!"

He dropped his face into the pillow behind her head and shuddered as he released his valuable fluid. Moira grunted unhappily but pitched her legs in the air and strained to make sure she didn't miss a drop. After all, that precious fluid had cost her an arm and a leg.

In the glass-encased overlook, Stori slapped her hand across the rocker knob on the light panel and the room was illuminated in brightness. She leaned forward to speak into the microphone. "As always, thank you for choosing us, Moira. Please put on the robe and your guide will direct you to my office. Good job Elijah. Retreat to your position until someone comes to get you."

She watched from the observation room as Moira pushed the large black man off of her body and swung her legs over the side of the bed. She was scowling and her lips were tight; Stori shook her head, tapping on the camera controls to zoom in closer on Moira's face. "What's wrong with you now, Miss Lady?" Stori sighed. Moira was never satisfied, she thought to herself and giggled softly. Moira was one of her highest-paying and regular clients but she was also one of the most difficult to deal with. She would show up weekly, waving around her flashy diamond jewelry without an appointment and demand service from one of their premium studs, all the while attempting to haggle a discount. Despite her swollen bank account, she was known for enjoying her appointment then freshening up and appearing at the front desk to lodge a complaint and demand that a portion of her bill be waived for the slightest complaint. They kept a file on her, filled with a myriad of complaints ranging from *"his toenails were too long and they kept scratching me"* to *"his armpits smelled like very bad."* The staff had been trained to alert Stori when Moira had a complaint, instead of automatically processing refunds.

She tapped on the keyboard and entered notes into the spreadsheet on the display screen. She already knew Moira was on her way to complain and try to bully her into some kind of credit. Dawn, her assistant, knocked and quickly entered the booth, pulling the door closed behind her.

"Stori, I'm sorry but Miss Moira wants to speak to you again," the skittish little redhead bounced on the soles of her shoes as she whispered across the booth.

Stori looked up and sighed. "What's her problem now, did she tell you?"

Dawn nodded. "She said she wasn't pleased - again."

Rolling her eyes, Stori tossed her auburn twists over her shoulder and spun back around in her chair to face the control board. "What a surprise. Send her to my office. I'll deal with her."

Moments later, the cloying smell of Moira's perfume filled the room as she sat scowling at Stori from across the desk.

"What can I do for you, Moira?" Stori lit a cigarette and inhaled deeply, then leaned back and peered at her client through the smoke wafting toward the ceiling.

"I'm not happy, Miss Stori. That certainly wasn't what I paid for - I expected much better. He was slow coming out of the gate! He seemed tired, are you not feeding them well?" demanded Moira.

"They get fed just fine. He's one of our premiums so he actually eats better than the others."

"When was he last checked by Dr. Papadeaux? Maybe his vitamin levels are low. Something is wrong," Moira sat with her legs crossed and she began nervously swinging the top leg back and forth, bumping the desk with her shoe.

Thunk. Thunk. Thunk.

If the intent was to irritate Stori and rush her to agreement, it wasn't going to work. Stori pretended to search the computer system but she was really dragging out Moira's time in hopes that she would just leave.

"Are you looking it up," Moira asked, her leg shaking harder.

"I'm trying, sorry, the network is running kind of slow today."

Moira shook her head. "This company gets way too much money from us clients to not have the best of everything."

"Oh, we have the best of everything. You must be pretty happy since you keep coming back," Stori forced a fake smile as she clicked around random areas of the screen.

"I keep coming back because I've spent hundreds of thousands of dollars and I'm still not a mother! Why am I not a mother, Stori? Can you answer that?"

Stori turned a stern face in her direction and folded her arms on the desk.

"Moira, you have been coming here for nearly two years. You were one of the first investors and then one of the first clients. I'm well aware that you've spent a ton of money on our services and although we do provide the finest of specimens...we can't seed infertile ground."

Moira's face turned beet red and she audibly gasped, but she stopped shaking her leg.

"I'm sorry, Miss Moira. I truly don't mean to be disrespectful, but it may be time for you to accept that this may not be right for you."

"I-I-I want my mixed baby!" Moira sputtered.

"I know, dear. And we've tried so hard. You've even been checked by not only our medical staff but also by your own. The problem isn't with our offerings. I'm so sorry."

Moira angrily stood and put her hands on her hips. Her face broke out in beads of sweat and she began to scream so loud that Dawn came rushing through the door in a panic.

"There's nothing wrong with ME! You had better get me some better men to pick from! I want my mixed baby and you'd better make it happen!"

Dawn stood protectively next to Stori and planted her eyes on Moira. "I think you should leave, Ma'am. Please don't make me call for Security."

"I'll leave. For now. But this isn't over. I'll be escalating my concerns. This company only exists to serve US. And if you can't do that, well, then maybe we need to make some changes to the operations around here."

Moira spun on her heel and walked out the door, leaving it swinging open to hit the back wall.

Dawn exhaled. "She's going to start trouble this time."

"Don't worry. She won't get far. We vote on the bill next week and all of this will be shut down anyway."

"I'm actually looking forward to it. I can go back to waitressing," Dawn said with a soft giggle.

Stori turned her attention back to the computer screen. "After the vote, this place will be turned into a nightclub. And I'm gonna be the first in line to shake my ass!"

In the column beneath Elijah's name, she checked the box to indicate a full completion, and entered specifics regarding his performance as she had witnessed. It took longer than usual for him to ejaculate, that concerned her so she clicked on the History tab to see if she could spot anything in Elijah's record that might be interfering with his ability to fuck. Dragging her finger across the touch screen, she viewed his health record that indicated a recent physical; his psychological evaluation was up to date and his diet and exercise charts had been updated earlier that morning. However, a glance at his work chart immediately highlighted the problem.

This was his 12th mating. And The Leopold Women's Designer Clinic and Hot Rock Spa had a firm policy of retiring all Bulls after 10 successful matings. There was no exception to that rule. It had been put into place mainly because licensing requirements included a clear deactivation agreement. However, there were other reasons why they limited the number of matings - they needed to control the number of children in the same area who shared the same genetic makeup. Once a stud reached the maximum mating, he was retired. For some odd reason, Elijah was still working.

Stori dialed *99 on the desk phone and spoke to the attendant that picked up.

"This is Stori Deringer. Access code 9j782cs. I need to retire Elijah Knox, service number 35452."

"Right away, Ms. Deringer."

"Thank you." Stori ended the call and stared into the darkness of the booth.

Moments later, the sound of gunshots rang through the building accentuated by a single scream as Elijah's service to the Leopold Women's Clinic was terminated.

Stori grabbed the trashcan from beneath her desk, brought it up to her face and vomited.

Minutes later, Stori chewed two antacid tablets and wiped tears from her eyes in the privacy of her small office. The decommissions always made her violently ill and she had never gotten used to it.

It was a brutal reminder that even though the front office dealt with affluent white women seeking designer beige babies (but not too beige), the back office of the business operated on death. The black men who registered to be part of the specimen pool were fully aware of what they were signing up for: $250,000 cash for their families, room, board and healthcare – as well as the opportunity to have unlimited unprotected sex – for the remainder of their lives. Which may be long or short, depending on how fertile their donations turned out to be. Some less productive men languished in the pool for months, enjoying the dining, entertainment and gym facilities, while the ones who hit their ten successful matings were terminated sooner.

To avoid putting them through the stress and trauma of knowing their expiration date, the men weren't kept informed of the number of successful fertilizations. Those final moments were handled as pleasant as possible, if one is able to be pleasant when they are about to put a bullet in your brain.

Thankfully, the tide was turning. The people would finally go to the polls and ban this heinous start-up industry before it took over the country and established clinics in every city. This sick desire to increase the population of mixed babies had finally angered enough of the right people and the nation would go to the polls and vote it down. It felt like they'd suffered under this regime for years but it had only been twelve months, but so many lives had been lost during that year, behind the walls of Leopold.

Stori thought back to the day she was lucky enough to hire into Leopold. It was soon after the *event*. That dreadful thing that happened and turned the world on its head. The world watched with baited breath as the so-called panel of leaders made the announcement that yes, we heard it right, our country would be moving forward with this abomination they called the "MB2056 Population Control Order". They were almost gleeful, snickering and holding back smiles, as they explained the conditions and the *'very attractive package'* offered to black men who stepped up to save the country.

Men drove far and wide to sign up for Leopold, the first and only center in the country. Truth be told, they wanted to fill the world with mixed babies as much as the white women wanted to possess them. The compensation package just gave them a smoke screen so they could pretend to be performing a civic duty.

Until people noticed that the men weren't returning home.

That's when Stori, podcaster and blogger - a born rebel and freedom fighter - decided to investigate and fight back.

From the *inside*.

Securing the interview was a piece of cake. She assimilated quite naturally with the top brass at the clinic because they saw her as one of them. They saw her fawn-toned skin, hazel eyes, and red boho mohawk with locs - they immediately relaxed, figuring she would understand and support the mission. When in fact, she found it disgusting and quite frankly, bordering on eugenics. And that's why she vowed to destroy it.

They walked Stori through the Operation room on her first day and she had to stop her hands from shaking from both excitement, nerves, and fear. It turned out to be smaller than she'd expected, in fact, she was quite disappointed to find that it was merely a room with several laptop computers

The woman moved around the operations room, waving her hand and barking instructions while Stori furiously scribbled on the pad of paper in her hand. She didn't dare ask the woman to slow down or repeat herself, so she wrote in shorthand and did her best to capture the key points, accentuating the page with quickly scribbled drawings for things she couldn't figure out how to describe.

The manager was huge - *stout*, as Stori's grandmother used to say. She was stuffed into a dark blue blazer and skirt that was straining to contain her girth. Her auburn hair piled into a perfect bun fitting for a prison warden, she stood at least six feet with broad shoulders that Stori imagined had stopped many a trespasser and protester from penetrating the security. She'd said her name was Something Tolliver, but the way she towered above the slightly demure Stori, she chose to mentally name her Gulliver, reminiscent of Gulliver's Travels. The thought almost made her giggle but she was afraid that if she did, the large woman might snap her throat with the precision of a warrior.

Gulliver stomped around the room, explaining the rules and giving Stori her directions as the newest Leopold employee. Stori's mind was racing, all of this information was good but she was in a hurry to get to the most important part, the part that made it all real.

The woman in the suit stopped in front of one of the display screens and held her identification badge to the barcode scanner. A green laser passed across the card and the screen unlocked, opening to a spreadsheet filled with rows of data. Stori stepped closer, still writing on her pad, and tried to read what was on the screen before Gulliver began moving the cursor to close the open windows. Stori was able to make out a list of names, contact information and titles in the far-right column before Gulliver clicked the X to close the window.

Employees? Stori wondered as she scribbled the letters "EMP file" on the paper.

Gulliver opened a new screen with a login fields on a blue background and Leopold logo. She turned to look at Stori.

"This screen is where you will log in daily to pull the numbers you'll need for your report."

Stori stepped closer. "I'm sorry, I didn't see how you got to that screen-"

"You'll need to swipe your badge first and then you click the icon on the desktop to get here," Gulliver paused and reached into the pocket of her blazer. "I almost forgot - you'll need this." She withdrew a lanyard with two plastic cards attached by a wire ring. One bore a smiling photo of Stori above a barcode, and the other was blank with only the Leopold logo and a numeric code.

Gulliver smiled and dropped the lanyard into Stori's outstretched hand. "Welcome to Leopold. One card will unlock the door for you each morning, and the other will log you into the computer system."

Stori's hand was trembling as she closed her fingers around the nylon cord. She bent her head forward and slipped the lanyard around her neck. Her body felt warm, as if there were heat radiating from the lanyard throughout her body.

"Don't lose that. Ever. Guard it with your life - literally," Gulliver said. The look on her face told Stori that she meant every word.

Later, Stori huddled in the storage house behind the stadium bleachers, designated by the team as the neutral meeting point.

"You know we're sitting ducks in here, right?" Drake whispered before Rena silenced him with a sharp glance.

"We won't be here long, Stori has a plan - go ahead, tell us what happened," Rena had to keep herself from bouncing with nervous energy.

Stori cleared her throat and leaned into the center of the huddle, the wooden beads around her throat clicked together as they hung to the floor.

She opened her palm to reveal a white plastic card resembling a credit card.

"What is it?" Drake fingered the edges of the card as it lay in Stori's hand. He flipped the white card over and revealed a wickedly-drawn L on the other side.

"It's a key pass that will unlock any door in the building. Well, it will unlock most doors.

I tried it on a few of the offices and they wouldn't open so I only have access to those that have been assigned to me. But it will get you inside on one of my days off."

Lillian gasped and covered her mouth, whispering through the openings in her fingers. "How did YOU get it?"

Stori grinned and reached down the front of her tee shirt, pulling up a lanyard attached to a laminated badge. "They gave your girl a JOB!"

She had to suppress her laughter for fear of the noise being heard outside of their hideout.

"Are you kidding me right now?" Rena picked up the ID badge and held it close to her face, trying to read it in the dim light of the moon. "Well, I'll be got-damn. They're dumber than I thought."

Stori giggled. "Yes, indeed. If I hang out long enough, they might promote me. I mean, I'm qualified, right?"

"Oh, you won't have to worry about a promotion," Rena took the key pass out of her hand and gazed at it lovingly. "There won't be anything left when I'm finished with them. I'm thinking...nightclub."

elle

Stori clutched the remote, her heart pounding as she watched the election results trickle in. The fate of millions of black men hung in the balance tonight. If the nationwide ban on breeding facilities passed, it would be a major victory. Although her heart felt as if it were beating in her throat, she almost giggled as she imagined thousands of angry, ovulating, white women lining up outside the federal building in protest, holding crude handmade placards that read, "WE DEMAND MIXED BABIES!"

Her team had campaigned fiercely for this ban. Since she was an employee of the very corporation about to be shuttered, she had to keep a private profile. But she had stolen and shared plenty of information with the team so they could plan their targets.

The numbers scrolling across the bottom of the screen tilted against the ban as more districts reported in. Stori swallowed hard. It was going to be very close; sickeningly close. Because even if the ban is confirmed, how do you move forward in a country that *almost* voted to keep it?

The doorbell rang and Stori jumped at the subsequent sound of the lock being turned; Rena let herself in with the key and dropped onto the couch beside her. She leaned in and planted a passionate kiss on Stori's lips and gave her a supportive rub on her back.

"I bought wine. I figured we'd need it either way tonight." She twisted open the top and took a swallow, passing the bottle to Stori.

Stori nodded, and accepted the bottle, keeping her eyes locked on the screen. She clutched Rena's hand tightly as the last few districts trickled in. Then the final tally appeared: 52% against the ban, 48% for it. The ban was defeated.

The ticker previewed a new headline that efforts would now in fact be ramping up to increase production in the facilities.

Stori's breath left her in a shuddering gasp.

Rena wrapped an arm around her shaking shoulders. "We fought so hard!"

Anger and sorrow battled inside Stori. The corporate farms always had more power. It wasn't right. She had to do something more.

Stori disentangled herself from Rena's embrace and stood up. "I can't let this be the end. We got soft. We were relying too much on a vote. A vote. History has taught us that it takes much more than that. We have to start a fucking fire!"

Rena stood up next to her, gulping from the wine bottle. "And I got the lighter, baby. But not tonight. Tonight, be gentle with yourself. We need you at your best."

Stori let the wise words sink in. She knew that if she allowed herself to be guided by her anger and pain, she might expose the entire mission. This loss hurt bitterly, but tomorrow her resolve would be stronger. She had to keep going to work each day and smiling and pretending that she was okay.

Rena was right - she needed rest tonight. Because tomorrow, she would begin planning an annihilation.

Author's note: I hope you enjoyed this preview! Be sure to sign up for my email and/or follow me to be updated when Seed (novella) is released!

Reviews Matter

If you enjoyed this book, would you please ?
You can simply click a star rating, or type a line
or two – either option is appreciated.

Did you know that you can leave a review on
Amazon even if you purchased this book directly from me? Yes, you can!! (Please consider
rating the book at both my website and Amazon.)

Thank you for reading!

About the Author

As a child, I realized that my entertainment choices leaned more toward ghosts and goblins than princesses and fairy godmothers. Now, I have a passion for weaving stories about monsters – both the kind that come from the pits of hell or the kind that may live right next door.

Find me. Follow me.

Follow me on my social networks to stay up to date on news, events, book releases and give-aways!

Official Website: www.kenyamossdyme.com
Facebook: kenya.mossdyme
TikTok: @kenyamossdyme
Instagram: kenyamossdyme
Youtube: @KenyaMossDyme

Catalog

Visit my Amazon Author page for the most updated catalog of my books!

Seed is available now!

"Wait," Myron whispered, struggling against the bonds. "I don't think I want to do this one."

Dr. Berkowitz offered the most terrifying smile Myron had ever seen. "What we want is irrelevant. What matters is what you can become, what we can achieve here. Right now."

www.ingramcontent.com/pod-product-compliance
Lightning Source LLC
Chambersburg PA
CBHW050338030726
47503CB00008B/2507